THE
JADE
GREEN
CATS

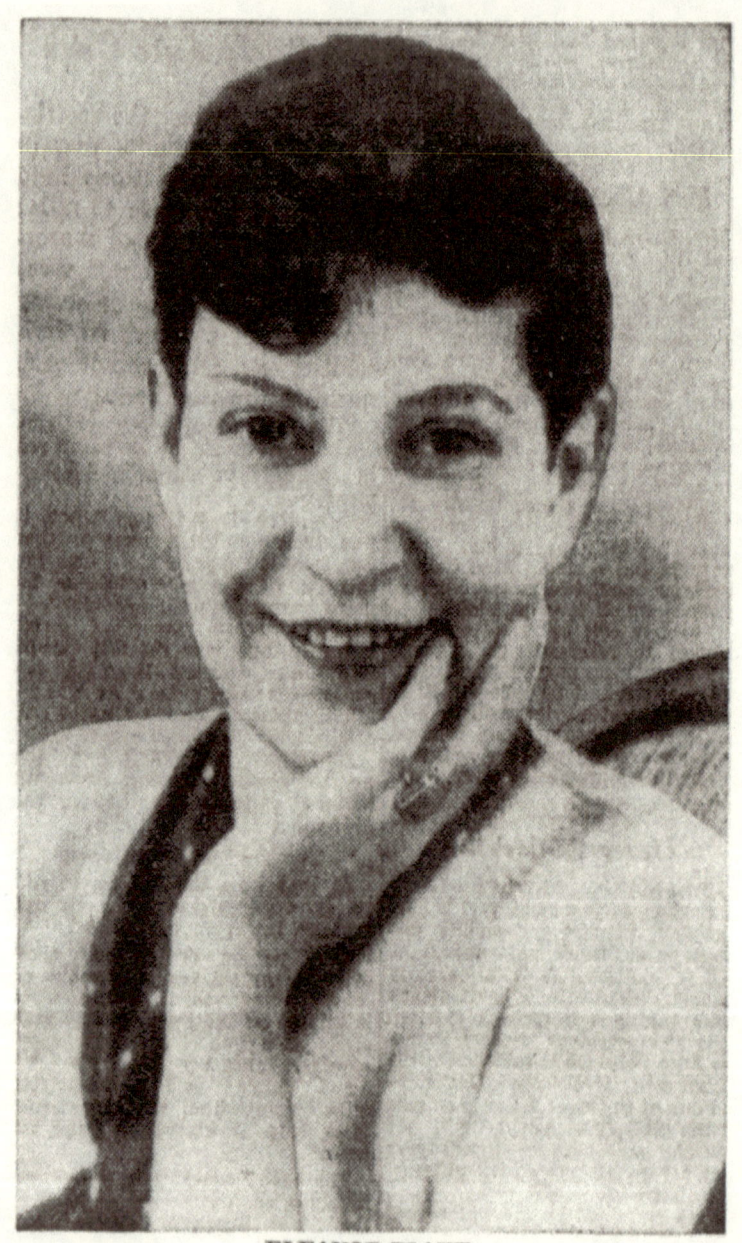

ELEANOR BLAKE

THE
JADE
GREEN
CATS

Eleanor Blake

COACHWHIP PUBLICATIONS
Greenville, Ohio

To Northport

The Jade Green Cats, Eleanor A. Blake
© 2022 Coachwhip Publications edition

First published 1931
Eleanor Blake, 1899-1952
CoachwhipBooks.com

ISBN 1-61646-537-9
ISBN-13 978-1-61646-537-7

1

A Date for Lunch

John Kymmerly stood just inside the revolving doors of the Tower building, and waited. He waited without patience and without resignation.

His head rested against the strip of gray-veined, polished marble that separated the two foyer windows of a shop devoted exclusively to the sale of sports wear for women. And it rested, in spite of the elevation of the window floor within, at a height somewhat greater than that of the taller of two wax models, both of which were engaged in holding a decidedly bad stance at golf. Which, reduced to simplicity, means that John Kymmerly was a good two inches over six feet tall—and rather disproportionately slender.

His face was young in its fresh color and in the soft quality of its close-shaved Saxon skin. But there were lines about his eyes—lines formed by wisdom and by watchfulness—and, marking the mouth as with parentheses, two creases which humor and scepticism had engraved. Blue and alert—the eyes—hard with rough knowledge, and they looked out from beneath the ramparts of his jutting brows on a world by which they couldn't be deceived.

Because Kym knew his stuff. He knew Chicago. He knew the traffic cops along Michigan, the lieutenants on duty at any watch in every headquarters station, and every

dick in the Bureau. He was on speaking terms with half
the city administration and had listened, in strict confidence, to a hundred stories about any and all of them that
couldn't possibly have been true if the other hundred he'd
heard—in equally strict confidence—had borne the faintest trace of verity. Because it's rather more than obvious
that two contradictions don't make a fact.

In short, Kym was hard-boiled—or thought he was—
which, in effect, amounts to the same thing. At any rate
he took his facts where he got them, thought about them
as little as possible, and condensed them into as few words
as would, with clarity, convey his meaning to a *Leader*
re-write man. He had his opinions of course, about this
and that member of the law-enforcement body, but he
aired them only in the already poisoned atmosphere of the
City Hall press room, or for the edification of Doc Yarrow
who was nearly always too tight to listen.

And to Dawn, of course. But about Dawn he preferred
not to think. He was still convinced—or so he told himself—that taking facts as you found them was the best policy—and girls as well as facts. And it was obviously true
that he'd broken a rule by unburdening himself to Dawn
on the subject of Hennery. Girls couldn't be trusted. Most
girls. But Dawn—well—that brought him to thinking
about her again and he'd decided not to.

Instead his mind swung back to Desplaines which he
had left not half an hour before to take his way eastward
along Madison. At Desplaines—that moldy, red brick
building that had served as headquarters for West Police
since long before he could remember, he had spent the last
two years in a state of armed neutrality with the *City News*
reporter who had followed him on the territory. True, it
wasn't actually his locality and it did, he supposed, belong
to Al Goodsol by right of inheritance. But good Lord!
He'd grown up there—from a standpoint of newspaper

work—played there, eaten there, slept there more often than not with his feet raised to the battered desk and his head supported in back-clasped hands.

They had quarreled continually—he and Al Goodsol—argued, ignored each other and finally, to prevent an open battle, Kym had retired to the hospital where he'd shared Doc Yarrow's quarters during the middle watch. Which, when Doc wasn't to the point of "out, out brief candle," had served him well enough. And at that he'd dictated more than one good murder over a telephone the mouthpiece of which had to be half-capped with his hand in order that the man on re-write wouldn't get Kymmerly and Shakespeare inextricably mixed.

Elliot on the *City News* had handled Kym's short, slangy sentences of revelation when Jim Colosimo had been found dead and with his diamond suspender clasps untouched. And, too, he'd taken Kym's word for it that the Franks murder was a kid's trick ("close your teeth on that, Elliot, and don't open your mouth until something turns up") and later had received, with an elation that was not in keeping with his usual imperturbability, Kym's drawling announcement that "they've got a boy wonder over at the Bureau who's handing out the gaff about a psychological experiment he's pulled off with a guy named Loeb—ye-ah, the Franks yarn."

Which are only two of the reasons why Elliot took Kym along with him when he went over to the *Leader* as City Editor, and why he turned Kym loose with a ninety dollar contract and orders—in the main—to find his own stuff.

It was in the dark, disorderly up-flight city room of the *Leader* that Kym had met Dawn Carson. And she'd succeeded in a surprisingly short time—considering that her objective had been Kym—in upsetting most of his ideas in regard to females. He'd discovered, among other things, that he couldn't judge her by back door standards, and that he couldn't dispose of her simply by classifying her as a woman. But the most that he'd actually granted himself—or her—up to the present, was a willingness to wait interminably in some prearranged public spot until she should appear.

He felt at that moment that he had already been waiting far longer than any reason could possibly excuse. If Dawn Carson thought that being sob-sister-in-chief to Chicago's most spectacular evening paper entitled her to undue consideration, she'd better wake up to the fact that that paper's best police reporter was entitled to a bit himself.

Strange faces continued to pass him in endless procession, and behind the swiftly moving traffic of the building the blurred background of Michigan avenue was veiled in a blinding downpour of summer rain. After all, he supposed, she might have got caught. But couldn't she take a cab? Dawn Carson never got caught. She always went where she wanted to go, achieved what she attempted, and took the resulting victory as a perfectly natural adjunct of Dawn Carson. Well—as for him—he'd be damned if . . .

His blond head, concentrated in the direction of the door, swung suddenly up.

"Hello, you," he called in a gruff voice as a small figure in a brief, black moire suit slid through.

"Hello, Kym," said Dawn, stamping her slipper-shod feet much as a cat shakes its paws if it has been forced into the contaminating vicinity of water.

"And I'm here to remark," Kym continued, eyeing the three drops of water that had managed to spot the crown of a satin hat between the door of a Checker and the foyer of the building, "that if you hadn't been on the job in another three minutes there'd been one lonesome lady waiting for a date."

"Me?" asked Dawn, incredulously. And then, revealing a sudden and wholly devastating dimple, she repeated, "Me-e, Kym?"

She planted both feet firmly together at a short distance from the marble wall and tilted her young body back. Her head, molded by the tight black of her hat rested against the stone wall at a point just even with Kym's broad chest. Her eyes, dark brown, and quick with a warm interest in all that life, so far, had offered her, shone beneath black brows.

"Me?" she asked again and then, "Oh, no, Kym. Anyway, you don't like to get wet."

Turning slightly she glanced up at the tawny head that rose so far above her own, studied a moment the clear blue of the self-deceiving eyes and asked,

"Love me, Kym?"

"Hmph!" said Kym, and took his pipe from his pocket. "Come on!"

But when he reached the door he woke suddenly to the fact of the rain and turned to face her laughter. He grinned.

"Sa-ay, Slim," he drawled when once again he had taken his place beside her, "we'll shelve for the moment any consideration of why you were so darned late, and take up another matter that seems, immediately, to be of more importance. It's just this—that my histrionic ability having, so far, been confined to a somewhat unusual rendition of Gungha Dinn or, on slightly more hilarious occasions, to my own interpretation of Mandalay . . ."

"Don't forget," said Slim, "to include 'A Woman is Only a Woman'."

"Admit that to the records. Anyway, what I'm getting at now is that the darndest slice of stuff keeps going around in my head. And I can't find where it lives.

"'And all that he felt at the back of his head
"'Were delphiniums (blue) and geraniums (red)!'

"Now what . . . ?'

"Gone in for book-reviewing?" asked Dawn who, meantime, was looking past him toward the door through which
the rain could be seen diminishing to a fine, warm mist.

"No!" His tone was scornful. "Picked up the fool thing on
Elliot's desk yesterday and that line caught. Now why . . . ?"

"Woman they're holding over at Desplaines raises delphiniums for a living, doesn't she—out northwest some
place?"

"Ye-ah, sure, but . . . There's the book-up! They found
a big bunch of faded blue flowers on the table in this man
Cartwright's office and I found—get me, Dawn—*I* found
four pots of red geraniums—smashed—on the floor of his
consulting room.

"But say," he interrupted himself, "how do you happen to know anything about the Thompson woman. I
thought . . ."

"If you'd been courteously inquisitive instead of merely
rude," Dawn returned, "I'd have told you that I was late
because I went over to Desplaines to try to get a story out
of her—hoping, incidentally, to run into you before you
left."

"They didn't let you see her, did they?"

"No—that's why I want to go back with you when we
get through eating. I couldn't budge Murphy—and Callahan continued to play checkers."

"And Hennery," Kym supplied, "has sure got the lock
on her. Still—something might be done . . ." he considered. "Rain's let up—let's go around the corner. Unless,"
he added, glancing at her with speculative and ironic eyes,
"you've decided to get high-hat and want to eat upstairs."

"No. I'd rather carry a tray."

"Right," said Kym. "We'll talk it over while we eat. I've
got some ideas on that killing and I want to submit 'em to
you for approval."

His tone was mocking, but as he turned to pilot her toward the Madison street door, his long austere fingers closed gently on her small arm. Together they joined the crowds and rounded the corner past the steps of the elevated to be swept along by the noon-hour rush of Wabash avenue.

Kym was head-high over the crowd as though fate had endowed him with the doubtful gift of being a little better than his fellow-men. While Dawn's small, quick-moving head was buried beneath a jostling mass of shoulders. There was that in her manner, a look in her shining eyes, that indicated her alert concern with all that went on about her. Mere superior stature, you must feel as you looked at Dawn, could never hope to cope with rapid intellect. And the warm smile that hovered, always, about the corners of her mouth echoed the tolerant humor with which her heart responded to the world. Dawn was inviolable by reason of her inability ever to take life too seriously.

At the doors of their pet cafeteria they turned in. They collected trays and slid them along the nickeled rail, gathering rolls and butter, passing up fish, deciding on roast beef which was always a good bet, and pausing to contemplate a pan of once-green asparagus that had been cooked to a gentle olive-drab.

"No," Dawn announced, "I'll take radishes for mine— or even pickles."

The stop for coffee gave Dawn her chance to get ahead and so to win by a nose the goal of the cashier's desk.

"On one," shouted Kym over her head.

"Two!" Dawn corrected in a voice much less powerful but, apparently, more convincing. As the girl behind the register dropped on her tray a small pink slip, her unre-laxing face softened to something that faintly resembled a smile.

"How do you get that way?" Kym asked irritably as they climbed the stairs to the relative seclusion of a balcony seat.

"Well—what's your contract? Mine's sixty and I share my rent."

"Ninety tops it."

"Yes, but that gives us four good feeds a month and four good shows—over and above cost of maintenance."

"All right—you win—this time."

They took a table in a far corner and for a few minutes there was only the companionable din of banging trays, clashing dishes, dropping cutlery, the shuffle of half-wet feet on the mosaic of the floors, the strident voices of the steamtable girls, and the subdued roar of the lunchtime gossip of several hundred office workers released from the enforced impersonality of routine and machines.

Dawn removed her food from her tray, arranged her knife and fork and spoon which, from the way in which she examined them, must have been of doubtful cleanliness, and slid the tray onto a nearby table.

"Kym," she said at last, "what have you got on Cartwright?"

"Just the facts," said Kym simply.

"Facts? Huh! You mean you've got the police report."

"Aided and abetted by my own not altogether unjustifiably famous ability to observe."

"Good! Did you go along and snoop with 'em? How'd you manage it?"

"Merely by being on time at the office."

"No-o-o! But quite aside from that, give me the dope, Kym. I've got to get the Thompson woman this afternoon if it means taking Murphy to the movies to pay for it. And I don't know a thing about her except that she raises flowers out northwest. Was she the doctor's sweetie—or only his stepmother?"

Kym buttered a roll.

2

The Cartwright Story Breaks

Kym bit into the roll he had buttered and leaned his elbows on the table in front of him. Dawn sighed gently, and with relief. The posture was sufficient indication—even without the pinpoint concentration of his eyes—that Kym was about to unburden himself of a host of well-accumulated facts. And this would save her a good deal of both time and energy that, otherwise, would have to be expended in unearthing the preliminaries.

"It is alleged," Kym began, elevating an eyebrow, "that Annie Thompson is a former patient of the deceased. Aside from that she's the last person this half-witted janitor saw go into the office. Added to which," he paused to regard the roll with distaste, "she's apparently contracted a most unfortunate habit of leaving things around. It's an error of judgment, Slim, for any woman to go depositing a package in a doctor's office. And it's a damned fool error—particularly in a city where the detective bureau is so entirely without sympathy for any alleged murderess of some fifty unattractive years—for that same woman to leave, in the reception room of a man who's going to be found murdered in the morning, an open package of pure arsenate of lead. Makes it too easy for the Bureau—and too hard for the woman. You know how that'd work out?"

Dawn nodded.

"I guess Cartwright was a nut all right—what kind I can't just make out. But he had a practice of sorts—mostly in cancer patients. We got all this dope from the janitor who said the Thompson woman had been coming in for nearly a year—almost as long as he'd been there. And that she usually had a boy with her—kid about fourteen.

"According to Watson—that's the janitor—the doc had extra office hours three nights a week, and helped Watson make out a skinny existence by paying him to run the elevator extra those nights from seven to ten. You know that old building, Slim, has about the only rope-pull elevator left in the world. Tuesdays, Thursdays and Saturdays, then, the old guy takes the doc's patients up after hours. And the Thompson woman had been a regular Thursday customer. She was there this Thursday all right, but she was there Friday, too, according to Watson—twice. The first time she brought the boy with her and left without him and when she came back later—a little before six—she stayed past the usual six-thirty release hour for this combination janitor-elevator-man, and so he trots along. Every time he'd pass the door—it's right opposite his shaft—he'd hear 'em at it."

"Hennery asked him had he taken anybody else up.

"Sure—he'd taken lots of people up.

"Was anybody else in the office when the Thompson woman was there, or was she alone with the doctor—barring the probable presence of the boy?

"But that the Watson person couldn't go so far as to say. He remembered the woman because he'd seen her often before, but he couldn't be expected, could he, to keep track of all the odds and ends that rode in his elevator of a day? And that was that.

"Well—about five-thirty this morning—and this is Saturday, Slim, Desplaines got a ring, and a woman who couldn't half talk English squealed into the phone. Said

she was over in the Umpire building—and there was a
dead man in 713.

"Emdig—he's the medic on the last watch—and a couple of men from the station ran over. But when they got
there the door to the elevator shaft was unlocked and the
elevator missing! So they had to puff up the seven flights—
comic interlude. In 713 they found five scrubwomen jab-
bering six different languages, and it was hard going to
sift out the one that discovered the corpse. But the corpse
was there all right—no mistake about that. Cartwright was
lying on the couch—couch, mind you—in his reception
room deader'n a door nail—and with his eyes popping out
of his head.

"As soon as they were sure it was true—and not a lot
of hooey—they called the Bureau. And as soon as they
called the Bureau, Emdig called me. I'd just ambled into
the office when Elliot got the phone. So it happened that
Hennery and I hot-footed it over at about the same time—
Hennery in the grey Pierce—and me in my trusty flats. At
that we got there together.

"The first person Hennery got hold of once he'd appeared on the scene, was this Watson person. There's a
bunch of keen minds over at the Bureau and Hennery,
being one of them, figures that the last guy that had anything official to do with the building the night before is
the one who'll know all about it—be able to clear it up
right away.

"I don't know how that outfit works in its mental make-
up, but it seems that Hennery must have thought old Watson stood around and watched it all happen, and then
went home for a quiet night's rest before coming back to
talk to the police about it. If he had, now . . . well . . . think
what a Desplaines street cop would have done to Watson!

"It didn't take long for Hennery—in spite of the heavy
cross-questioning he always stages—to get out of Watson

what he knew. Because he didn't know a lot. Nature hadn't endowed him with much of a bean to begin with and he wasn't any good at faking details he hadn't seen.

"He's a squat, swarthy little man with bowed legs, and a pair of arms that's too long for his body—arms like an ape. I guess Saturday isn't his day for a shave—or else he'd been waked up too soon by the visiting officers of the law. Anyway, he had a thick, black stubble over the lower part of his face and his hair drooped across his eyes so he had to look out through it like a dirty poodle.

"Honest, Dawn, if he hadn't been so doggone dumb, and I'd been Hennery, I'd arrested him on suspicion just for looking like that. And I'd arrested him, too, for making such a damned fool of himself over that antique elevator. Because when he found it was gone he just about went crazy.

"'I left the cage at the bottom of the shaft!' he kept shouting. 'I left it at the bottom of the shaft. Where's it gone?'

"'Probably to the top,' Emdig told him with rare good sense. So then the whole tribe of us clattered up three more flights. And sure enough—there's the rackety contraption resting in peace at the top. It lets out on the tenth floor and there's a flight of steps that opens off a small door and goes up half a flight or so to the roof.

"Lord! What a row! That fixes everything for Hennery. The door was open and there was a good set of footprints on the combination of gravel and asphalt that paved the roof. Well—that asphalt had baked soft yesterday and was in good condition to preserve prints for the police department this morning.

"But there was just one trouble with 'em: they led backward! Yep—the blamed prints began at the edge of the roof nearest the fire-escape right up to the trap that lets onto the stairs—and into the building.

"Hennery couldn't figure that out. It just about broke his heart. He couldn't tie it up with the elevator. It didn't reason. If the guy that had committed the murder (and who else could have done it?) had used the elevator as a means of entrance to the seventh floor, and escape to the tenth, then he couldn't have used it as a means of exit unless he'd walked backward to the edge of the roof. And Hennery wouldn't believe any fool'd do that. On the other hand, if he'd come in over the roof, he couldn't have used the elevator for any logical purpose unless he'd gone down ten flights after it, run it up to create a false impression and then made his leisurely way down to the front entrance among odds and ends of scrubwomen. Hennery didn't like it—not a bit. But he made a note about it, anyway—for future reference."

Kym lighted a cigarette and then continued,

"After all this heavy deliberation on the part of the chief, we clattered down again to have another look at the corpse. The Watson person—safely in tow—couldn't tell us where the Thompson woman lived—and didn't even know her name—then.

"It's possible the doctor's books might have done us some good—if we could have laid our hands on them. But there wasn't a trace of books or papers. The office looked like it had been all cleaned up to be left for a while. The safe and the instrument cases were locked, and the desk was cleared. And beside it was a gladstone bag.

"After we'd taken all this in we went back to have a look at the corpse. He'd been a tallish man, and thin as a split rail. He had sandy hair—the red skin that goes with it—and a hawk nose. On his chin was a thinnish beard of the kind they used to call Van Dyke—when they wore 'em. I haven't seen one for so long, it's a wonder I remember. Gave him a foreign look, somehow, though I couldn't figure his country, and his name's the sort anybody could have picked up.

"But there were two things about him I couldn't help noticing. One was that his arms and fingers were the longest, narrowest set I've ever seen on a human being—not barring mine. And the other was that his eyes—pale, milk-blue eyes—were nearly jumping out of his head. How a man could go along with a pair of eyes like that—and live . . ."

"But he didn't," Dawn put in.

"No—that's true. But the pop eyes didn't have anything to do with his death as far as anybody could see. He hadn't been strangled. They couldn't have had anything to do with it unless . . . but no . . . that's too far-fetched."

"What is?"

"Nothing stirring. I'm not going to air a fool theory and then see it popping up in a sob-story as the authentic conjecture of Annie Thompson. See?" He grinned.

So did Dawn. "All right, Kym. You'll unburden yourself some day."

"Sure, after you're through getting interviews on the thing.

"Fact is," he went back to his story, "there wasn't a reason that anybody could see why he was dead. There wasn't a mark on him—but he'd died hard. His mouth was partly open and his tongue stuck out—and one hand had closed tight on the side of the couch.

"'Poison!' Hennery decided in that divine-right voice he can put on when nobody else can figure out a thing.

"But Emdig had sense enough to shut his mouth tight, shake his head a little, and say nothing. Ye-ah—Emdig has a lot of brains—when it comes to holding his job.

"But nothing was mussed up anywhere near the body. Half way across the room there was a big mahogany table, and on the floor beside it was lying a broken bowl. It was kind of a nice bowl, too. You'd probably say it was rare or something—Chinese.

"'What's all this white stuff?' Hennery wanted to know. It was scattered on the rug around the bowl and it looked like table salt. Felt like it, too. And a big round spot a little to one side looked as though it had been scorched. Hennery made a packet of a piece of paper and took some of the white dope away with him. He's the greatest guy I ever saw for making notes and collecting facts which he's afterwards too ignorant or too lazy to relate.

"While he was busy in there I wandered into the next room where we'd been looking for papers a while before. The bag's what struck my eye, and I asked Hennery if he'd examined it. He didn't take the trouble to answer me, but opened it up while I stood and looked on—I wouldn't touch a fly if it was on a case where Hennery was working. The bag had been packed for a trip, apparently, and then considerably mussed up. The clothes had all been pulled out, I guess, and then stuffed back without much care for how they went in the second time. And in the bottom, wrapped up in the shirt of a pair of striped pajamas, was a funny-looking cast iron cat. Honest! It looked like it had been one of a pair of bookends and at first I thought it was carved jade—not bad looking. But when I stooped down beside Hennery to get a good squint at it I saw it was cast metal or some sort covered with a dull green enamel. Hennery shook it and put it back again. Then, without so much as his customary glance of disgust in my direction, he walked out of the room.

"That gave me the clear field I'd been wanting. I looked around. It was an ordinary sort of consulting room—a little shabbier than some—with two windows. The west light looked out over a vacant quarter-block where a new building was being put up, and the north window opened on a fire-escape that descended to an alley. The north pane was shattered—something that Hennery'd made a great fuss about first thing. And underneath each window were two broken flower pots. All four of them had held red geraniums, and the flowers were beginning to wilt. But the earth had been shaken out of their roots and it was spread all over the floor—even and thin—as though some-body'd been sifting it pretty thoroughly. And that made me remember that there'd been some dirt—regular black garden soil—on the pajama shirt the cat was wrapped in.

"And not a dick in the place had hooked the two to-gether. They'd gone around examining the fire escape and picking up broken pieces of glass, and getting pop-eyed over the bowl in the reception room, but even the chief had kicked the flower pots out of the way as he went around looking for evidence.

"Now listen, girl, I'm no genius, but I've dug up more funny facts by sticking to the idea that necessity's the mother of a lot of things besides invention. And I'm hold-ing onto those pots of red geraniums—in my head—until somebody proves to me that Dr. Cartwright was in the habit of making mud pies as an indoor sport—or I prove that he wasn't.

"I was hunched down on the floor thinking some such deep and valuable thoughts as these when somebody in the other room gave a yelp, and I jumped to my full six feet two and a bit more. Two steps of my good long legs brought me to the other room, and from where I lit I could see the outer door.

"Standing just inside the office was a tall, gaunt wom-an of sixty or so with a flat hat perched on the top of her bony face. The face was seamed, wrinkled, lined and weathered with worry, and her eyes were half-crazy with what I could only take to be fright.

"Half-way across the room from her the Watson person was jumping up and down like a fool, and shouting,

"'That's her! That's her!'

"'You old idiot!' she said, her voice, for all her crazy looks, steady enough, 'what are you doing up here? I've come to see you a-purpose. Why aren't you running your creaky, old cage—and where's it at?'

"She looked around at the lot of us, but for some reason her eyes didn't light on the corpse just then. I suppose our quiet made her nervous. Anyway she turned on Watson again, and shrieked,

"'Where's the doctor gone to? That's what I want to know. Where's the doctor gone to?"

3

Annie Thompson

"We stood there like a pack of fools," Kym continued, "like a dumbfounded pack of fools. And Hennery with his mouth open half an inch looking for all the world like something they'd just let out of Dunning.

"Here was the woman we wanted to get hold of, the woman whose name we didn't even know, and whose address we couldn't discover—the woman the Watson person had last heard in the doctor's office the night before—the woman Hennery had counted on having to spend a couple of weeks and at least six special men in finding—the woman I'd figured would make a column a day while they looked for her—walking into us of her own accord, and then asking us,

"'Where's the doctor gone to?'

"It made even the Watson person shut up for a minute, but he came to before the rest of us and began jumping up and down again—hollering,

"'Where's the doctor gone to? Where's the doctor gone to? Fine person you are to be asking "where's the doctor gone to?"'"

Kym shook his head.

"That was less than three hours ago, Slim, and I haven't got over it yet. I thought I'd gone batty. I thought the whole darned works'd go batty and we'd all start up with a chorus of 'where's the doctor gone to?'—with slow music.

"Because with that Hennery pulls out his most sarcastic voice and joins in the chant.

"'Oh yes,' he chirps, 'where's the doctor gone to?'

"I couldn't stand it, Slim. I walked across in front of Emdig and swung in ahead of Watson. And I stood there like the hero of a melodrama—which is what I was beginning to feel like—and pointed with my long, bony finger to the body that was lying on the couch.

"She turned, that gaunt, queer-looking party in the gray calico dress, and when it had come home to her that the thing she was looking at was the body of the man she had come to find—Dawn, she grinned. There's no other name for it. Her wide, narrow-lipped mouth stretched into a horrible smile. She looked at that corpse as though her hungry heart could never take in enough of the sight before her. She stared and stared. Then slowly the grin relaxed, and a look of fear took its place. She turned so that she stood facing the rest of us, looked from one to another, and then her eyes fastened on Watson.

"'Where's Sandy, then?' The question was a scream, and the force of it seemed the motive power behind her sudden rush across the room. She clutched Watson's shoulders in her clawlike hands and shook him as though he'd been a boy. 'What have you done with him—the two of you?'

"Then as though a veil had been dropped suddenly over her face, the expression changed. Fear again—but this time a fear that I can describe only as impersonal—a blank, naked terror. She stared at us all again and started toward the couch where the doctor's body lay—then she let out a shriek that made even Hennery jump, and started running from the room.

"That brought 'em all to life. Emdig made a lunge for her; one of the men from the station jumped in front of her, and Hennery grabbed her by the back of her dress. Only Watson and I stood back—Watson because he was shaking like a leaf over in a corner where he'd slumped into a chair, and I because I couldn't for the life of me have touched her. She didn't seem human enough to touch. She was possessed—gone crazy—and I couldn't work any sense into the plot.

"But where I fall down is where Hennery shines. We'd make a swell team if we'd work together—instead of ever-lastingly gagging each other. Where my imagination stumps me by putting me in the other fellow's boots, Hennery's all safe because he hasn't any imagination. He always keeps cool. He never loses his head. Because even when he seems to be losing it, he's doing it for effect. And, as a result, he always gets his man—nearly always.

"Hennery's two hundred pounds of bulk man was turned on the woman. He shook his mop of thick, black hair in her face. He talked straight at her in the sort of low, booming voice I've heard him use to get the truth out of a black-hander—and there's no truth in 'em. He motioned her to a chair with one of his fat hands. He said,

"'No, you don't. You'll stay right here until you've answered a few questions to my satisfaction. First, what's your name?'

"At that she stared at him as though she'd really seen him for the first time. She gave another look at the body on the green velvet couch, glanced back at Hennery and all of a sudden sat down in the chair. She folded her hands in her lap—still—and the crazy mouth that had been screaming a minute before, was closed as tight as a trap. The eyes that had stared at all of us as though she'd kill us for a cent were fixed on the wall in front of her.

"'Annie Thompson,' she said at last.

"Hennery threw back his coat so that the long, gold chain that festoons his front stood out like a shackle, thrust his hands in his pockets and stood in front of her, his head bent and his cold, black eyes fastened on her.

"'Annie Thompson,' he began, 'I suppose, by the way, that it's Mrs.—huh?'

"He seemed to take her silence for agreement.

"'Mrs. Thompson,' he went on, 'the body of Dr. Cartwright was found here early this morning and you, I am sorry to say, were the last person known to have been here last night. I hope you can give us some information that will help clear the matter up. I'll just ask you a few questions now and if you can give answers that are satisfactory I'll be glad to let you go about your business.'

"He smiled agreeably—for Hennery. But Annie Thompson continued to stare at the wall in front of her.

"'Mrs. Thompson, you visited the doctor in this, office yesterday afternoon, didn't you? And again last night?' He waited.

"'I asked you,' he said impatiently, 'to verify the facts that the elevator man has given us as to your presence in this office yesterday?' Again he waited.

"'Mrs. Thompson,' his voice was raised, 'were you or were you not in this office last night?

"'Answer me!'

"He swung away from her, walked the length of the room and returned.

"'All right. All right.' He turned again, walked over to a small table where a package, broken open, lay scattering a fine gray powder on the mahogany, and swung back to Annie Thompson, carrying some of the stuff in his hands.

"She half rose from her chair, reached out a hand, drew back in fury and consternation, subsided into her grim silence.

"'I thought so,' said Hennery. 'So you recognize it, do you? Is it yours? Did you bring it here? Forgot it—did you? Hah! Careless! Arsenate of lead's nothing to play a fool's trick with. What were you doing with it?'

"She clung to the arms of her chair with desperate hands, dropped her head for a moment and then, once more, raised it to stare at the opposite wall.

"'So you were here,' Hennery kept badgering her. 'Better admit it now. It'll save you trouble later on. And you brought the poison, didn't you?'

"It seemed to me that her head involuntarily gave a little shake of denial, righted itself at once and grew rigid again. She continued to stare.

"'Better tell your story, Annie, and get it out of your system. You'll feel better—and it'll go easier with you, too. First place—what did you two quarrel about—you and the doctor?' His tone was almost conversational.

"She lifted her head at that, looked at Hennery, glanced across at Watson and her eyes, before they took up once more their interminable staring at the wall, held an expression of scorn.

"'You'll admit you were quarrelling. What was it all about? Money? Was it a long fight—been going on some time? Was he trying to do you—or had you beat your bill?

"'Hm! Won't talk—huh? Well—we'll see . . .'

"Meantime Emdig had picked up the bunch of faded flowers that had been lying beside the package of poison, and as Hennery turned away from Annie Thompson, Emdig walked toward her.

"'So you raise flowers, Mrs. Thompson. Do you go in for anything besides delphinium? Roses?'

"She nodded.

"'I've just taken to the roses this last year, and they don't do so well.'

"The calm of her voice was a surprise.

"'And you've been spraying 'em—eh? What's the arsenate for—slugs?'

"'Yes, and I use it with sulphur for the mildew, too. I didn't really know . . . Cartwright—he told me what stuff to get. If only . . .' She closed her lips firmly once more and shifted her gaze from that of Emdig.

"'If only what, Annie? If only you hadn't come up here?'

"'No! No! If only I had before . . . no . . . you'll not have another word out of me.'

"'You know about it then,' Hennery cut in. 'You're not trying to deny that you left the poison here in the afternoon and . . . and what . . . you'd better tell us the rest. Come on—you'll be held as accessory after the fact if you're not sewed up on any other charge—unless you come clean. When you do, you can go home.'

"'I don't want to go home,' Annie Thompson cried. 'I don't care if I never go home again. I only want . . .' She turned to glare at Watson. 'Where's Sandy? You know— and you're hiding him from me. Tell me or I'll . . . where's Sandy?'

"'And who's Sandy?' asked Hennery who, whatever his faults, is always quick in the uptake.

"'Sandy's her boy—her daft kid she's so crazy over.' It was Watson's voice—come back from the dead for all we'd been hearing of it before.

"'So-o!' said Hennery, as though he'd discovered who'd killed cock robin.

"But Emdig, who was standing on the side-lines and was expected to stay there, cut in suddenly,

"'Mr. Watson, I thought you didn't know this woman's name—or where she lives. Yet it seems you know a lot about her when it suits you.'

"Watson looked from one to another of us like a scared rat, and finally spoke in Hennery's direction.

"'I didn't want to get her in trouble,' he mumbled.

"'Trouble!' she spat it out. 'Trouble's the last thing would stop you where I was concerned. And what's more, you know a deal more than I know about this mess. You was in with the doctor on some crooked sort of a deal—that I do know—and you're shaking in your boots now for fear it'll be found out, now your boss is dead. You . . .'

"'Annie,' said Hennery suddenly, smoothly, 'does this arsenate belong to you?'

"'Yes,' she answered sullenly.

"'Did you leave it here yesterday?'

"'No.'

"'Then who did?'

"She stayed quiet—wouldn't open her mouth again.

"'Answer me!' Hennery demanded impatiently, 'or I'll have to take you to the station.'

"But the woman sat there with a hard look in her eyes and wouldn't budge. She had a secret and she'd made up her mind she was going to keep it.

"Hennery badgered her a while longer, and Emdig took a turn or two with his soft-pedal stuff but they couldn't—either one of them—get another word out of her. Finally they took her along and locked her up in the hospital at Desplaines. You'll find her there—unless Hennery's taken her over to the Bureau by now—but I don't think you can get at her—or get a story out of her if you do.

"She's a queer bird, but I think, at that, that Hennery's on the wrong track. I don't know—I don't know . . ."

Dawn touched his hand.

"Have they got the goods on her, Kym?" she asked in a small, strained voice.

"Sure they've got the goods on her," he said, killing his cigarette in the dregs of his coffee, "but it doesn't mean anything."

4

Desplaines

The fact that the Desplaines street police station was built of red brick, and that it had grown bilious under years of Chicago soot, didn't affect Dawn in the least. The fact that it was dirty where it wasn't bleak, that it had housed, at one time or another, a goodly portion of Chicago's bums and more than its reasonable share of Chicago's crooks, left her spirit unruffled. She didn't even mind that it smelled.

Because she was used to it, and used, also, to a more than faint aroma of romance that had clung to it, undeviatingly, since the first night that she had, in the disorder of the station hospital, shared rye-bread sandwiches and beer with Kym.

"Hello," she said to Lieutenant Murphy whose hard, seamed face greeted her from behind the desk. His wise, brown eyes twinkled, and his friendly mouth, compressed habitually into a narrow watchfulness, relaxed to a welcoming smile.

"Well, well—how are you, Slim? Haven't seen you around for a couple o' weeks. What's the matter with you and the Dutchman?"

"Not a thing, Lieutenant Murphy. He'll be tagging in in another minute—stopped to talk to Emdig, I guess, before he goes off duty. Is Doc Yarrow on yet?"

The lieutenant's face sobered.

"Ye-ah—he's on," he said, "but Yarrow's got hypo-activity today—you know."

"Sure," she agreed, "but that'll wear off."

"Not fast enough to suit Hennery. Hennery's mad and he's goin' hot on this Cartwright job. And Doc'll find it pretty bad riding for a while after he wakes up to the fact that there's been a murder in Desplaines territory. You know, Slim, the doc's got a pretty good head when it comes to figuring out morbid psychology from a basis of abnormal physiology. Get what I mean?"

"Where is she?" asked Slim.

The officer's face hardened, and his lips narrowed to a secretive slit.

"You can't see her," he said, and turned at once to a minute examination of his books.

"Hm!" The saving humor of her nature manifested itself by the slightest of slight crinklings at the outer corners of her eyes. "The *Leader* wants a story on her this afternoon—you know—the 'kind that only Dawn Carson can write.'"

He had the grace to grin at that but he followed the grin with a negative movement of his head.

"Orders," he said with all the power and grandeur of his office behind the simple word, "from the Bureau."

"But where'm I going to eat my supper?"

"Well—you might try Myer's. Of course it isn't what it once was, Slim," he sighed, "but Loo can still put a good salad together—bacon on it—chopped."

"I'll wait for Kym."

She strolled into the large, dark hall that opened out of the front office and glanced into the press room. Al Goodsol was sitting there with his feet on the desk and a telephone in his hands. ". . . not a thing," he was saying. "They've got her under lock and they won't give out a word until the Chief's lined up some more dope. Murphy told me they found the other package of poison out at the old girl's place—and she's got a boy up her sleeve—mother's darling and all the rest. What? Well . . . Northwest isn't my territory. And they haven't brought him in. What? They haven't done a damned thing but . . . Oh—a-all right."

He slammed down the receiver and reached for an outside phone.

"Mansfield 47420," he shouted angrily. And Dawn scribbled the number on the margin of her *Daily News*.

Then she turned her attention to the other side of the broad, dark, low-ceilinged room where two men in uniform sat playing checkers. To a thick plank, rough-planed and painted red, the sliced-off top of a battered checkerboard had been tacked. Grosvenor and Callahan were each seated on what once had been a chair. The back rungs of that upon which Callahan sat had been wrenched out in some ancient, long-forgotten battle, while Grosvenor balanced with a skill that was the product of long habit, on the remaining three legs of another.

They were silent.

"Hello," said Dawn.

Neither glanced up. Neither spoke. Dawn remained standing beside Grosvenor, her eyes fastened on his opponent. Grosvenor crowned a king.

"And two!" shouted Callahan triumphantly, making a double jump with a commoner.

"Hello, Slim," he then observed expansively. "What's your trouble?"

"Do I look as though I had a trouble?"

"Sure you do. Why else would I be asking you?"

"Well . . ." said Slim, "it's that woman." She indicated the closed door of the hospital with a nod of her head.

"Want a story on her and Murphy won't let you have it—huh? Well—he's got his orders. Still—why don't you pick on Hennery—direct?"

"Hennery doesn't like me."

"It's your own fault—working for a sheet that's agin the administration."

"No," said Dawn promptly, "it's my own fault—pure and simple. I don't like Hennery."

Callahan grinned. "Oh! They'll let up on her after while. Maybe Kym can do something for you."

"That's what I figured." And she pulled up a third battered remnant of a chair and sat beside them—sinking her chin in her hands.

"Whose game is it?"

"Mine," said Grosvenor shortly.

"But it's goin' to be mine." And Callahan closed his teeth firmly on the stem of his pipe.

Dawn had patiently watched Grosvenor's quiet satisfaction register over two games and Callahan's exuberant triumph react to one before the corners of her alert eyes had caught sight, once more, of Kym's long, easy stride.

He passed all three with only a glance in her direction and a quick toss of his head toward the press room. She rose at once and dropping one quick, wicked eyelid at Callahan walked lightly and rapidly across the room.

"Sorry, Goodsol," said Kym to the slim, dark boy who occupied the only chair in the room, "they won't let us in the Doc's office, so we'll have to stay with you a while. You know Miss Carson . . ." His manner was elaborate.

Al Goodsol nodded and took his feet off the desk. He was watching Kym with an alert and angry expression of frustration and disgust.

"Got anything new on Cartwright?" he asked at last.

Kym took his pipe from his pocket, held its bowl affectionately in the palm of his hand for a moment, filled its well-charred chamber with tobacco from a red can, and slowly lit it. His eyes were half closed, their expression contemplative and remote, and when he opened them wide to look at the *City News* reporter, the clear blue of their encountering gaze was wholly innocent, entirely candid.

"Not a thing," he said. "How's it go with you?"

And only then did he look down at the folded copy of the *News* which Dawn had dropped into his lap. On the margin running from the point where she had noted the telephone number which Goodsol had called to the top of the paper she had scribbled hastily: "Al called this number after he talked with the desk. What's it all about?"

The *City News* man glanced quickly at the two, seemed to decide with an equal quickness that discretion was the better part of valor, and said with an air of casual indifference:

"Rotten! Long as Hennery keeps her sewed up, nothing'll break."

Kym leaned forward and, with the long arm that seemed capable of reaching to the moon, lifted a telephone from the desk.

"Mansfield 47420," he suggested to the operator. His manner indicated that he hoped she would agree.

Goodsol straightened up suddenly and leaned forward.

"It's no good, Kymmerly, there's nobody there."

"So I hear," said Kym, "but I think I'll just ask Information to get me the name and address on that unless . . . unless you'd rather tell me yourself."

"All right," said Goodsol unwillingly. "It doesn't amount to much. The old girl in there's got an offspring—boy about fourteen. And she's keepin' her mouth shut about him something elegant. The Chief can't get a word out of her except that he's a good boy and he's not mixed up in this. Aside from that, she won't answer questions. She'll talk about herself—tells a straight enough story until she comes to that poison. Then she gets balled up.

"That—and the boy. That's what Hennery's keeping her locked up for. And she'd better know he's hard. He'll keep her there on rye bread for a week unless she decides to open up. I'll bet he won't even let her get into an ambulance for the Bureau or the County Jail—much less the Revere House—unless she peeps. Monotony's the idea, I guess."

"Ye-ah?" drawled Kym. "And what's that got to do with the Mansfield number?"

"That's the old lady's home phone," Al Goodsol grumbled.

"You don't deserve it," Kym remarked as he swung to the door in two easy strides, "but I'll give you a tip. Keep your eyes on the boy and forget the old lady."

"Nice of you, Kym," Dawn observed as they walked toward the hospital. "Did you mean it?"

He grinned. "It's as good a guess as any."

"And now we're going to get a look at Annie Thompson."

"Kym! You darling!"

Dawn looked up at him with the glance of wondering admiration which some men would have given a good deal to win.

But Kym only said, "Applesauce!" and thrust his pipe savagely between his teeth.

Then he flung open the door of the hospital and held it for her to enter.

Doc Yarrow was reclining in an arm chair that had degenerated from a noble life at sea. Lieutenant Murphy had inherited it from his father who had been a car-ferry captain during the war and had passed it on to the hospital only after deciding that he liked all three of the men who held watches in that post. It had a foot-rest, two broad arms, a caned back and seat, and was painted Kelly green. Doc Yarrow lay in it now—and snored.

"Hi!" shouted Kym. "Want a drink?"

The doc sat up with an amazing abruptness, looked quickly around in a dazed manner, glanced at Dawn, nodded, and reached a sudden arm out in Kym's direction.

"'S all right, Kym, I need it."

Kym poured two fingers of Scotch from a bottle which he took from the doctor's safe, and held it out to Yarrow.

Almost at once the man showed unmistakable signs of life.

"Now look here, Doc," said Kym, leaning forward and tapping the doctor's thick knee with a thin finger, "I'm a friend of yours. That's so—isn't it?"

"Sure," said the doctor. "Give me another drink. I need it."

"You don't. What you need's a shock. And I'm going to give it to you."

The doctor continued to look indifferent.

"Where's the key to that room?" Kym indicated a closed door that let into the east wall.

Doc Yarrow began feeling feebly in his clothes. When he didn't find it he pawed at his desk. Gradually a look of consternation spread over his face.

"Emdig must o' forgot to leave it," he said at last.

"No," said Kym, "Emdig didn't forget to leave it. Hennery took it."

This was the shock that the middle watch medic had needed. He sat up and looked apprehensively toward the door.

"No, again," said Kym. "They haven't locked a stiff in there. It's only a woman—alive—and they think they've got the goods on her. I wonder what you'll say when you see her—raises delphiniums for a living. Right, Dawn?"

"The first time," said Dawn.

On Doc Yarrow's face the lax expression was being replaced by one of craft and determination.

"Kym," he said at last, "I've got to have another drink—you know."

"Yep," said Kym, "I think you do—now."

Yarrow took the drink, opened the glass doors of his instrument case, extracted a large roll of adhesive tape and, from the bottom of the tin which had held it, took a key.

"Always knew that'd come in handy some time," he remarked as he wavered toward the door. "Hennery needs teachin'. If that guy thinks bein' Chief lets him put it over on me . . . Kym . . . you're my frien'—so's the li'l girl—any frien' o' yours . . ."

"Ye-ah, that's all right, Doc," Kym interrupted.

"Well—if you two'll keep your traps shut about it, we'll go in and have a talk with the lady—Thompson—huh?"

He grinned triumphantly and inserted the key in the lock.

Less than an hour later Dawn was feeding yellow sheets of onion skin paper into a typewriter and at two-thirty she handed her story to Elliot with the comment:

"Got it by a stunt. Maybe you'd better hold it until we've had time to give Hennery a copy. I think it'll bring him across with an O. K. Don't you?"

"Sure thing," said Elliot—and then ignored her. For he'd picked up her copy and was reading.

"Geraniums!" he read. *"May the doctor's soul burn in Hell for them!"*

5

On Being a Cub

Kym sat in the press room at Desplaines with his feet resting on Al Goodsol's desk. Above his head a Republican campaign poster looked steadily, and with total unconcern, at an indifferent portrait of the Democratic candidate for the same office that occupied a good portion of the opposite wall. And on the third, facing the dirty window that let in the even dirtier light of a narrow side street there were tacked four reprints from the rogues gallery, and a flash-light picture of the murdered proprietor of a north-side delicatessen.

Kym gazed at these with pride. They had been his contribution, some two years before, to the decorative scheme of the room. He'd selected, on a rainy afternoon when the atmosphere had particularly encouraged a morbid taste, the four worst looking crooks he could find. Two had cauliflower ears, one a dislocated nose, and the fourth was minus an eye. They were all hard, all dirty and one of them had been tight when he sat. In each group the profile looked with an expression varying from simple disgust to surly resignation, on his own front-face. And beneath them all the prints of their fingers spread fanlike, in a gay design.

Kym dropped his eyes from a contemplation of what, in a sense, had been his own handiwork, to raise them again

for a continued survey of Al Goodsol's desk. Kym rarely
moved, in even the least important of his enterprises,
until his plan of action had been carefully perfected. In
this way he saved for such occasions as demanded it his
precious store of energy.

For some five minutes, now, his eyes had searched, at
intervals, the darkest recesses of the battered, roll-top
desk. Finally he decided that what he thought he saw he
really did see and, in accordance with the decision, leaned
forward and took from its semi-obscurity the object of his
interest.

"Now where," Kym asked the rogues, the corpse, and
the portraits of two rival candidates, "did he lay hands on
that?"

He turned in his hands the jade-green cat he'd last seen
in Dr. Cartwright's packed gladstone bag, tipped it upside
down, shook it, and redeposited it in front of him.

"And what," he continued, "does he want with it?"

He sat and thought for several minutes.

"Besides which," he finally questioned, tilting his chair
forward and dropping his feet to the floor, "what the hell
is it all about?"

He paused to listen. He'd heard the door bang for the
hundredth time in an hour. He'd heard the inner doors
swing open and then close with a scraping contact as
their edges joined again. He'd heard rapid, nervous steps
approach the press room.

"Hello, Goodsol," he called before the *City News*
reporter had time to reach the door.

"Hello, Kymmerly." The boy dropped into a chair and
thrust his hands into his trousers' pockets. He was a small-
er man than Kym, shorter and dark. And because he was
a cub reporter of some scant twenty years on a salary that
had stubbornly stayed at thirty dollars during a discour-
aging number of months, there was nearly always hovering

about his eyes a look of semi-fright. Today he was worse than usual.

"Where'd you get that thing?" Kym asked him suddenly in a voice no noisier than ordinary, indicating, with the stem of his pipe, the jade-green cat that sat bolt upright on the desk before him.

Al Goodsol jumped.

"What? That?"

"Ye-ah, ye-ah, you heard me." Kym crammed the pipe into his mouth.

"Oh that . . ." said Al Goodsol.

Kym eyed him with hostility and returned to a contemplation of the cat.

"Well—you see—I happened to be in Yarrow's office around noon and . . ."

"It wasn't Yarrow's office around noon. It was Emdig's. And don't tell me Emdig gave it to you, because he wouldn't."

The cub was irritated.

"I didn't say Emdig gave it to me. I said I was in the hospital around noon—when Hennery brought the Thompson woman in. He had a bag with him—Cartwright's I guess—and I began nosing around in it."

"You would," Kym announced, and then, in all fairness was forced to admit, "but then—so did I. That's where you found the cat . . ."

"Yes, thought it'd make a good paper weight. Ever see it before?"

"Sure," said Kym, "I ran across it the same way you did—only I don't happen to be in with Hennery."

He bit into his pipe.

"By the way," he said, "who's this Bothwell person?"

Kym fired the question suddenly, removing the pipe from between his teeth long enough to speak and then

reinserting it while his eyes closed the better to allow his
ears to take in what might follow.

The forward legs of Al Goodsol's chair came down with
a bang, and Al Goodsol coughed.

"Ye-ah," said Kym, "who's this Bothwell person you've
been telling Pollidick about?"

"Oh, he's just a guy."

"What kind of a guy?"

"A teacher—professor, if you'd rather."

"I'd rather nothing. I only want the dope on the Bothwell man."

He leaned forward.

"Listen here, Goodsol," he said, crossing his long arms
on the desk in front of him, and nursing the bowl of his
pipe lovingly in the palm of his hand, "if I'm not wrong, I
broke you in on this territory, and I've helped you out in
half a dozen scrapes."

He emphasized his remarks by tapping Goodsol on the
back of the hand with the stem of his pipe."

"I don't believe you hate me so much as you've just got
it in for me. Why?"

Al Goodsol squirmed.

"The Chief doesn't like you."

"Who? Hennery?" Kym roared.

"Well—yes," said Goodsol, his eyes dropping before
the other's amazed stare.

"You don't tell me, Goodsol, you don't tell me. Now I
thought . . ."

And then Kym started to laugh. His laugh was loud,
long and infectious. Before he'd finished, two sergeants
and the first watch medic had joined them.

"What the hell?" asked Callahan.

Kym waved at him with his pipe.

"It's all right, Lieutenant. This bird and me—we're just
getting acquainted." Then to Goodsol:

"Listen, kid, the first thing I got lammed into me when I was training was that I was working for a newspaper and not for the dicks. Dicks may come and dicks may go, but the press goes on forever—something like that. If you can stay in with 'em, all right. If you can't—without selling your soul—tell 'em to sell theirs. As for Hennery—say, I can do more for you in ten minutes than the Chief can do for you in a year—unless you're thinking of joining the force."

His tone changed abruptly. "Now snap out of it. Who's this Bothwell person?"

"Well," said Goodsol, hesitation still restricting the boyish frankness of his face, "he's a professor of psychology."

"And . . ."

"He was a good friend of Cartwright's."

"Such a good friend," said Kym, his eyes narrowing, "that he bumped him off."

A look of horror and negation passed over the frank face of Al Goodsol.

"Oh, no," he said, "he's come clean to help us out."

"How clean? And who's he going to help?"

"Hennery—that's why . . ."

"O-o-oh! So that's it. Hennery thought he'd keep that little card up his sleeve, did he?"

This fact seemed to amuse Kym out of all proportion to its obvious value.

"What's the Bothwell person's yarn?"

The *City News* cub looked thoughtfully at his fingernails, glanced up at Kym, eyed furtively the door that stood open at his back. He moved uncomfortably in his chair, shifted his feet and finally removed from a crushed and nearly empty packet a bedraggled cigarette. He lighted it, watched for a moment the smoke that rose in a lazy cloud, and finally leaned forward.

"Well," he said in a voice that was subdued and some-what frightened, "you see it's this way: he was a friend of the Doc's—best friend he had according to his story —known him for years. But he found out—just by acci-dent—that the doctor was planning to leave Chicago late last night for a long trip. Took him by surprise—shocked him—hurt him quite a lot—to know that his best friend had planned to leave without letting him know a thing about it. So he went straight up to Cartwright's office and Cartwright explained everything—told him why he was leaving so suddenly—said he'd intended to get in touch with him, and asked him to come back that night for a last party. That was about four o'clock yesterday afternoon. He went back all right—about seven-thirty—and his wife with him. They broke up between ten and eleven and he says Cartwright was well and in his right mind when they left—waved 'em good-bye from the landing."

"All to the berries—huh? Any signs of the Thompson woman on the premises?"

"Why—a—no—don't believe so. Can't remember whether Hennery asked him."

"He wouldn't. It'd spoil his catch. He'll hold her till he gets somebody else to lay his hands on. And if he doesn't . . .

"What was the Bothwell person doing there? What was the party all about? Who else was there to say good-bye to the guy that was all lined up to croak? And—has Bothwell got any witnesses?"

"Just his wife," was all the bewildered cub could man-age to answer to the fusillade of questions. "They've got a date with Hennery for tomorrow morning. Said he'd tell him all about it then. So Hennery let him go."

"Let him go, did he? Ye-ah—that sounds like Hennery. No wonder he doesn't like me. I don't like his methods. He's the kind of a guy that sees a black bass in the water while he's trying to get a dog-fish off the hook. He'd like the bass, all right, but he figures he's got the dog-fish and he might miss catching the bass. So far the Thompson woman's the dog-fish. But how'd the bass happen to swim his way?"

"Huh?" said Goodsol.

"Where's this bird Bothwell land in from? How'd they find him? Where'd they get the dope on him?"

"Oh," said Goodsol with relief, "he just walked into the Bureau and said he'd come to tell what he knew."

Kym sat up suddenly.

"So he's that kind of a guy—is he? Who's hiding behind his skirts?"

This put the cub on the defensive.

"He told a straight enough story. Said Cartwright was heading for Europe and it kind of broke him up to find out he was being left out in the cold on the information."

"Any tears?"

"What? Oh! Well . . . he admitted it cut into some research they'd been doing together—and he suggested they get together that night and have a little party."

"Parties," said Kym, "have a way of being bad. What about the wife?"

"She didn't come down with him, but he said she'd be along tomorrow."

"And the elevator. Did anybody happen to mention the elevator to Bothwell?"

"Oh, yes," said Al Goodsol eagerly. "Hennery asked him about it the last thing and he said he noticed, particularly, that it was at the bottom of the shaft because his wife said something about wishing they knew how to run it when they came in at seven-thirty and, as they reached the main floor on their way home, she laughed and grumbled about it again."

"Hm!" said Kym. "And that's the end of the tale—ye-ah?"

He smoked for several minutes while his eyes narrowed to ruminative slits.

"And tomorrow morning," he said at last, "is when this story is due to break. Tomorrow morning, however, is some eighteen hours off. Meantime there's one newspaper in town that'd like to scare up a little dope on the Cartwright murder. Now listen here, Al, you stick to me—see? Hennery can't do anything but get you in wrong with the administration—and that won't touch your pay envelope. While I happen to know there's a job sort of half open on the *Leader*—and it isn't territory, either. Get me?"

Al Goodsol apparently got him.

"Now you just slip me the address of Bothwell. Hennery can think I swiped it while he was asleep or picked it up on a handy street corner. I'll see you get the whole story—the whole story, mind, just exactly one hour after the *Leader* sets up its first scare-head."

In less than ten minutes Kym was on an Evanston express, fingering in the right pocket of his coat the rather bulky outlines of a cat that, from its dragging weight on the seams of his pocket, gave every evidence of being made of lead.

6

The Professor Comes Clean

"Good morning!"

The voice was startling because it was unexpected. But the intonation seemed wholly fitting to the high Victorian room with its two tall windows looking east and south, and its walls austerely paneled in dark oak. The speech was dry, precise and dignified, and since it issued from a direction in which no door existed, its owner, Kym decided, must have been there when the small, neat maid first showed him into the room with the assurance that the professor would see him at once.

But Kym had been particularly careful, so he thought, to make certain that the room held no occupant besides himself, and his leisured examination of the book which he was now holding had been accomplished, until this moment, without self-consciousness. He tried—with how much success he could not be certain—to retain the manner of unworried ease as he turned in the direction of the voice.

But even a complete right-about-face did not reveal to him at once the source of that greeting, the tones of which had been edged with irony. He stared, blinking, into the broad beam of light that cut the room across. For while the shifting shadows of the elms on the lawn outside subdued the light that entered through the east window, that from the south was unbroken by any shade.

He stared, and as he stared a hand obtruded, was thrust with an effect that was nothing short of startling into that golden bar of sundown which a million tiny spots of colored dust drifted and flowed on. Kym ignored the hand while his eyes sought its owner. He shifted his enchanted gaze so that he saw above and beyond the blinding light, and as his eyes grew accustomed to the shadow he made out the figure of a man. At this he accepted the hand and, in a voice that was challenging in that it was unusually distinct and more than ordinarily clear, he asked:

"Professor Bothwell?"

"Professor Bothwell," the man assured him, and then rose and stepped forward so that his thin body, too, was for a moment transfigured by the sun. He indicated a chair, and his ascetic face warming to a smile, he said:

"Sit down, won't you? You'll find cigarettes in that red box. I don't smoke, but my wife does. Very convenient for any of my guests . . ."

He had a way of indicating criticism, contempt, a slight disdain, by the finest of shadings in tone, by the mere choice of a word. Kym found him objectionable and conveyed the fact by accentuating his own habitually, blunt manner.

"I'm from the *Leader*," he said.

"So I should judge," returned the professor, his eyes dropping—could it be by accident?—to Kym's exuberant tie.

Kym's eyes narrowed.

"The *Leader*," he said, pausing to light a cigarette and so gain time in which to size up his opponent, "is a good paper if you happen to like it. Which I rather bet you don't."

"Well—no," still in the subtly condemnatory tone.

A spontaneous emotional statement of preference can be entirely acceptable even when you don't agree with it, thought Kym; but this business of carefully balanced judgment, carefully balanced speech, was not to his taste.

"However," the man was going on, "I assume that it sometimes finds its way into the house, for I see the maid kindling a fire with it occasionally."

He indicated an open grate.

"Through," said Kym good-naturedly, "the back door."

"Ah—yes—yes. Still—hostilities aside . . ."

The professor's narrow lips relaxed and his eyes took on, for perhaps a moment, a faint trace of geniality.

"I'm here," Kym said flatly in an effort to get the situation in his own hands, "to get your views on the murder of Dr. Cartwright. You seem to have been mixed up in it more or less."

"Mixed up? Well hardly. And why do you—and your friends the policemen . . ."

"If you mean dicks," Kym interrupted, "they're not my friends."

"What I was about to ask you," the professor continued, undisturbed, "is why you insist on calling it a murder? Has any evidence been found to substantiate such a theory?"

"No direct evidence. But when a man's found dead with no witnesses to give the cause of death, there's usually an investigation."

"Ah—yes—yes. But such an investigation is often fruitless. My friend—the doctor—was a strange man, a very strange man. He was given to sudden enthusiasm, sudden violences, and as is often true in such cases, to sudden moods of depression and discouragement. I should not be too surprised if it were found that Amos had taken his own life. There were circumstances . . ."

The professor paused to consider the wisdom of making such revelations.

Kym leapt into the gap.

"What circumstances?" he asked.

The professor raised his eyebrows.

"It did not occur to me," he said, "that I was on the stand. It does not occur to me now that, purely as a representative of the press, you have any right to question me at all. You've been talking to Mr. Hennery, of course. I had his word for it, in consideration of the fact that I came forward at once with a good deal of helpful and totally unsolicited information, that he would not let the papers get hold of it until I was ready to be quoted. I find it irritating."

He coughed dryly.

"Hennery hasn't peeped," said Kym. "I got my dope from another bird who happened to be around when you told your yarn. Even the walls of that damned Bureau have ears. Fact is Hennery'd rather boil in oil than give me a line on any story that breaks. He doesn't like me—or the *Leader* either."

"As to the latter," said the professor, "I can't say that I blame him. However, I'm sufficiently intelligent, my dear Mr.—ah . . ."

"Kymmerly."

"Thank you—yes—my dear Mr. Kymmerly—to realize that what the *Leader* does not get directly it frequently contrives to get by—you would doubtless prefer the word 'intuition' in this case . . ."

Kym grinned.

"Very well, then. Intuition is a feminine trait and therefore not always wholly reliable. I prefer, of course, to provide you with the story as it occurred. It might, in that case," he seemed to dwell on the idea for a moment before continuing, "just possibly have a chance of appearing, initially at least, in an unperverted form. It would be interesting to preserve for posterity . . ."

"Professor Bothwell," said Kym quickly, but very pleasantly indeed, "at what time did you first see Dr. Cartwright on Friday?"

The professor rested his elbows on the arms of his chair and brought his hands together immediately in front of his face. Slowly he clasped them and, during the remainder of the brief hour of his stay, Kym watched those nervous fingers closing and unclosing in a rhythm that was as regular as the motion of precise, scholastic thought.

"I should prefer," Professor Bothwell answered, "to tell it in my own way. It will have, then, perhaps, more the meaning which I see behind it and infinitely more the meaning which I wish it to convey."

Kym nodded.

"In the first place I should like to give you some idea of the relationship that existed between myself and the man whose dead body was found in his office yesterday morning. We were friends in no ordinary sense. We were, in fact, friends whose tie consisted mainly in a protracted controversy. Occasionally it took the form of experiment and once, at least, it forced us both to publication.

"The book which you were examining when I spoke to you" (he smiled as though in reminiscence of Kym's embarrassment on that occasion) "was, I believe, entitled, 'A Chemical Theory of Soul' and it bears the name of Amos Cartwright. The volume that you will find next to it—if you will be so good—no, the green one—ah, thank you—yes—is my answer: 'The Soul—a Logical Entity.'

"The two books are the result of our mutual—although antagonistic—research. Dr. Cartwright was engaged, constantly, in demonstrating a theory which concerns itself primarily with the impossibility of the survival of personality after death. I, on the other hand, have held firmly to the orthodox opinion that the soul of man is not subject to decay.

"Now it is in the nature of man to be vain of that which he honors with his regard. And in the case of Amos and myself it was inevitable that we should be egotists when it came to matters of the mind. That the doctor had occupied himself with chemicals and with the physical concerns of human beings makes it not at all surprising that he should seize on a purely materialistic conception of the universe and of man's spirit."

Kym shifted his long legs so that he might find more room in which to stretch. Then he selected a cigarette from the red box which stood on the table at his elbow and, while lighting it, eyed the professor with complete distrust. The professor was telling an entertaining story, enjoying himself immensely with the spinning of a few fine threads of theories, but the warp and woof of the tale that Kym had come to hear had not yet begun to show on the loom.

"That's very interesting, Professor," he said, "but . . ."

"Yes, yes, I know."

He clasped and then unclasped the long, thin, agitated hands which remained, meanwhile, raised to the level of his face. His thin lips were pursed in an expression of concerned preoccupation.

"Amos had," he finally admitted, "an open mind on the subject. He was always more ready to experiment than I. Not only in his own trend—mind you—but he helped me, frequently, to carry out such ideas as I might develop. He was far more courageous than I when it came to demonstration.

"I am," he paused, seemed to hesitate, "I am essentially a coward in the face of death. This fact Amos invariably attributed to what he called my stubborn tenacity to an outworn belief. He was convinced that once I should embrace his certainty that man is but the flame of a candle to be snuffed out by the wind of death, I would lose that shuddering horror of the actuality.

"I—I—Mr. Kymmerly, this is a strange admission from a grown man—from an old man, I suppose your youth would label me, but—I have never been to a funeral."

His head dropped forward on his raised hands; he trembled almost imperceptibly.

"I could not bear to see Amos now," he said at last, raising his head to look at Kym, his face gone quite white. "It is the spirit that I treasure and the spirit, I feel sure, that triumphs over the death of the body. I shall not go to the funeral. Amos, I know, would be the last to expect it of me. I hope you understand."

He paused again, and the hands that were raised before his face shook as he clasped them.

"Yesterday afternoon—Friday—" he continued at last, "at somewhere in the neighborhood of four o'clock—it may have been a trifle after that—I was strolling along Michigan Avenue in the cool shadows of the buildings. I'd barely reached Adams and was looking, as I invariably do, at the stone lions that seem with such unfortunate success to guard the portals of our domain of art, when I bumped into an old acquaintance. And when I say that I bumped into him I mean it in the literal sense. With my eyes fixed on the front of the Institute I did not, of course, see the man who was hurrying toward me with his head buried in the collar of that ridiculous coat. But when I looked up after the impact, a little doubtful whether to apologize or be indignant, I knew him at once.

"He'd been a schoolmate of mine in Vienna and had known Amos well at that time, too. But he was the last person in the world I'd expected to see on an August afternoon in Chicago.

"I greeted him, though, as any man would greet an old acquaintance and only remarked, in passing, that I was surprised to see him in a city so far from the scene of what I knew to be his activities. He granted that my surprise was justified, especially as the trip had been rather sudden and unexpected to himself. He was carrying a heavy bag and glanced down at it.

"'Would you mind walking on with me? I have an important engagement at four o'clock,' he said.

"He told me then, while I hurried along beside him at a pace which I found uncomfortably rapid for an August afternoon, that he had only recently arrived in town from New York and would be returning on a night train. He expected Amos Cartwright to return with him.

"This startled me, my dear Mr. Kymmerly, almost beyond belief. I had seen Amos only the day before and he had mentioned no such trip. I offered, at once, to go on to the office with him and we continued up Madison Street together.

"I made rather a joke, in the face of his continued, self-absorbed silence, of the fact that he was wearing a coat with an astrakhan collar. But his sense of humor had never been a strong point, even in his student days, and what little he had ever possessed seemed to have deserted him before the circumstances that had driven him to cross the ocean only to return at once."

"The ocean?" Kym interrupted. "I thought you said he'd come in from New York."

"Yes, yes," Professor Bothwell said hastily, "so I did. I had forgotten entirely that you did not know he had come by way of New York from Europe—one of the small principalities. He was rather short with me about the coat. He said:

"'Yes, but it's cold enough once you're on the water, and I always contrive to keep my luggage about my person. It's safer.'

"When I reached the doctor's offices I realized, from the manner with which he greeted me, that Amos had expected him and that my presence was a hindrance to a discussion of their plans.

"I was as brief as possible and only learned that Amos was not only leaving for New York with our friend but was planning to sail on the first ship, by way of Amsterdam. Passage had been engaged for both of them.

"There must have been a betraying expression of regret on my face, for Amos suggested that we all get together for a final meeting that night. I believe he mentioned that a community of interests bound us together. He thought it might be interesting to have a final experimental séance before his departure. His train didn't leave until 11:30 and there'd be plenty of time to call up all the ghosts we knew before then.

"I left shortly after."

"Where did you say he was headed for—what country in Europe?" Kym asked.

"I don't recall," said the professor, smiling blandly, "having mentioned his destination in any more definite way than that. Europe, I feel, is enough. And I hardly consider the question pertinent."

Kym shrugged.

"I hope that the one I am about to ask will seem somewhat more pertinent. Did you notice anyone in the outer office when you passed through?"

"Y-yes." The professor hesitated. Then, with reluctance, he admitted, "That simple boy of Annie Thompson's was sitting in the big armchair holding a package in his arms, and a great spray of delphinium—beautiful shade. I remember, now, thinking how pitiful he looked."

"And when did you come back for your ghost party?"

"It was somewhat in the neighborhood of seven-thirty, I believe. We made it early because we'd have to break up in time for Amos to catch his train."

"And then? Was the boy there then?"

"No—certainly not."

"Nor the mother? Any sign of her?"

"No. Nothing—that is—except the package the boy'd been holding. It was standing on a small table at one side of the reception room, broken open, and a greyish powder had run from it all over the floor. The poison—yes—it must have been the poison."

Kym leaned forward eagerly.

"The package was broken when you saw it at seven-thirty?"

"Why, yes. Yes."

"Did anybody mention it? Ask Cartwright about it?"

"No-o, I don't think it was referred to. Nothing exactly startling in it. One is apt to see all sorts of chemicals around a doctor's office, you know. The only thing that has made me recall it at all is that I noticed a similar package in the boy's arms earlier in the day. I couldn't even swear it was the same. Simply—the two were not connected in my mind. I attach very little importance to this poison theory anyway. The police are making a great deal too much noise before the verdict of the coroner's physician has been received."

"Granted," said Kym, "and now . . ."

The oak door that led into the hall swung open and the small, quick figure of a woman—almost a girl—stepped into the room. She looked from one to the other of them, walked to the table and, taking a cigarette from the red lacquered box, lit it.

"Amelia," said the professor, "this is Mr. Kymmerly, a representative of the—ah—press. That is to say, my dear, a reporter for the *Leader*. Mr. Kymmerly, Mrs. Bothwell."

Kym stumbled to his feet.

The girl turned away from him, but only after a charming glance from beneath long lashes.

"Alton," she addressed her husband, "I'll tell Mr. Kymmerly anything else he wants to know for your detested *Leader*. Karl Meisterberg is waiting to see you in the living room. And I should imagine, too, that he was rather hot."

7

The Professor's Wife

Karl Meisterberg, it occurred to Kym, was doubtless of much less importance in the life of an aspiring reporter than the small, brilliant figure who had come to announce his arrival. Immediately on the departure of her husband, who must be nearly twice her age, she had perched herself on the arm of the chair which he had so recently occupied and sat swinging slim and pleasant legs that were clothed in gunmetal chiffon. Kym noticed narrow-slippered feet, a dress of some thin stuff that echoed the Chinese red of her lacquered box, and a small, well-poised head, whose shapeliness was accentuated by the glossy cap of her short, dark hair.

She smoked nervously for several minutes and then looked up, her black, inquiring eyes encountering Kym's blue ones with a distinct challenge.

"You have a suspicion," she said. "What is it?"

"No." He laughed. "You've guessed wrong to begin with. I'm all at sea on this story. I haven't yet discovered anybody who seems to have had any real reason for bumping the old guy off."

"Annie Thompson?" she inquired.

"Rats!" said Kym. "She happened to be there at a time that makes it convenient for Hennery to use her as meat to the wolves. I don't think that even Hennery'll be able

57

to hold her much longer. Public opinion's a pack of hungry animals but it can't be stopped long with a dry bone
to chew. Much as he doesn't like to, Hennery'll have to do
some work on this case before he's through."

She nodded a quick, decisive little motion of the smooth
head that conveyed to Kym her approval.

"You're intelligent," she decided; "and, what's more
valuable still, sufficiently ironic. I've half a mind— No!"

She swung down from the arm of the chair and crossed
the room. From the red lacquered box she took and lit
another cigarette, then walked toward the east window
and looked out across the quiet lawn. Suddenly she turned
back.

"I wonder," she said, "if I can trust you? I think I can
if you're sufficiently sold on my integrity. And yet—and
yet I can't tell you enough about myself—about the whole
situation—to make you believe in me from a basis of facts.
Oh, dear! Now I'm getting all balled up. Mr. Kymmerly,"
she came directly toward Kym and stood looking up at him,
for by this time he had risen and was facing her, "look at
me—right straight at me. Am I an honest woman?"

Kym looked, long and unhesitatingly. He was being
challenged; his capacity to judge human nature was being
tested; his very honor, in a sense, was being put to trial.
He suspected that the woman was trying to use him, was
transforming him with that dangerous alchemy that only
women know. And yet . . . He suddenly became very mat-
ter-of-fact.

"I don't know," he answered bluntly. "But if what you're
after is this: Can I keep my mouth shut, I'll answer you
directly. Yes. And what's more I will. I'm a reporter for the
Leader, but in spite of the connection that's so objectionable to your husband, I'm a human being. Fire away."

"I want to ask a question," she began abruptly. "And I
want you to know that it's very important, indeed. Stop

and think—be quite sure before you answer me. And
don't—don't tell me 'no,' if there's the least doubt in your
mind."

She drew at her cigarette and, after a moment, breathed
out a thin cloud of smoke.

"What's more I'll be able to ask you only if you'll swear
you'll keep the question to yourself—tell nobody that I've
asked it."

Kym nodded.

"Very well, then. Did you see in the doctor's office a
pair of book-ends in the shape of two jade green cats?"

Kym kept himself from making an audible sign of surprise only by an effort of his will. The foolish object of
his light interest would seem to be turning into the focal
point of the whole mystery. Only—the professor's wife
referred to a pair of cats, while he'd come across only a
single one. He hesitated and then, for answer, drew from
the pocket of his coat the cat he'd carried from the press
room at Desplaines.

"O-oh!"

Did her voice convey astonishment, consternation,
shock? Kym decided quickly that what it most indicated
was relief, infinite relief.

She leaned forward eagerly and was about to seize it
when Kym's long fingers closed over the head.

"No—you don't," he said. "That cat belongs to the
estate of the late Dr. Amos Cartwright. And if it's so all-
fired important to you as it seems to be, you'd better go
about getting it through the regular channels. I'll admit
I've no right to it, and it only came into my hands by way
of a couple of other people who had no right to it and who
decided, apparently, that it had no value and would not be
missed from among the effects of the dead. The thing for
me to do with it in the circumstances is to turn it over, at
once, to Hennery and tell him what's it about."

"No! No! You mustn't do that. You mustn't. You don't understand. That would ruin everything. Besides," a crafty look came into her eyes, "you've given me your word that you'd tell nothing of what's gone on between us. And if you turn it over without explanation it'll go through the same process of being lost. And it mustn't be lost. It mustn't. You don't understand."

She was twisting her hands now, walking frantically up and down the room.

"Where's the other cat?" she asked at last.

"I don't know. This is the only one I ever saw. If there's a pair I'm ignorant of it."

"You'd have hard going to prove it if I ever made a point of using it against you," she said. "You don't know what you're playing with. That cat can get you into trouble or keep you out of it. You'll find yourself in it head over ears if you attempt to give it up. If you do what you threaten to do, I'll give the whole story to the authorities, and the whole story'll stir up a hornets' nest that'll sting people clear across the ocean."

She pointed a finger dramatically toward the east. "And if I should do that, the burden of proof would rest with you. You'd have to produce the other cat or be accused of . . . Mr. Kymmerly, you haven't the faintest conception of what a dreadful thing you'd be accused. Please—please— believe me."

There were tears in her eyes.

"And what about the relatives?" Kym asked lamely. "Amos Cartwright's family must have some claim on an object or—as you say—on a pair of objects that are so damned important."

"He has no relatives." Her voice held relief. This, after the complications of the last few moments, was apparently a simple and clarifying issue. "There is no one who has any claim on him unless it would be Annie Thompson.

And Annie Thompson—oh! will you believe me?—Annie Thompson wouldn't have the faintest idea of what to do with the cats if she had them. Nobody . . . Mr. Kymmerly you must take me on faith . . ."

She was reduced, again, to an abject distress, her eyes lifted pleadingly—very soft, very childlike.

"And you must help me. You must help me to find the other cat." Suddenly her face cleared and her expression, so lately downcast, desperate, was one of hope. "I'll tell you," she said eagerly, "we'll make the cat a hostage to my honesty. Do you rent a safety deposit box at any bank?"

Kym grinned.

"No," he said, "it's easy to see you don't know any reporters."

She reached in a purse and handed him a bill.

"Rent one," she said, "rent it in your own name. I must trust you. Put the cat in your deposit box until we've found the other. Then—I hope—by that time things will be in such a state that I'll be able to secure their release from you without any question as to my integrity. Do you agree?"

"On the one condition," said Kym, "that you'll release me from all previous promises if the life of any person is endangered by my keeping them there. I won't see Annie Thompson hanged if I discover that the cats have any bearing on her guilt or innocence."

"Yes, yes," she said, "of course. But that would be absurd."

"And what's more," said Kym, "this secrecy business has got to work both ways. Two other people besides myself have seen the cat: Hennery and the *City News* reporter on West. Goodsol knows I have it. As long as nothing comes to light about it I'll not be questioned. But if the issue appears you'll have to handle it on the square—understand?"

She nodded.

"And now," said Kym, "I'd like to ask you a question or two before I leave. Were there any drinks served at this farewell party the doctor staged?"

"Yes," she replied at once. "My husband drinks very little, but the doctor gave us all a crême-de-menthe in recognition of Alton's liking for cordials."

"And the bowl. There was a Chinese affair smashed on the floor. Do you know anything about that?"

She laughed with relief.

"Oh that!" she said. "That was done to give true atmosphere to the séance. Did you ever see salt that's been saturated with wood alcohol set on fire? We used to do it when we were youngsters, a regular stunt on Hallowe'en. It gives a ghastly greenish light, makes your skin look bilious, and creates a perfect setting for ghosts. It was set in the middle of the table and, of course, with the first lift it slid to the floor."

"The first lift?" Kym looked skeptical.

"Why, of course," she said. "When Alton's pet spirits raised two legs of the table preparatory to his counting out the alphabet, the bowl naturally slid off." Her tone was normal, her expression that of one who refers to the ordinary affairs of life.

"And do you really believe . . ." Kym began, but was interrupted by the voice of the professor who called to his wife from the outer hall.

"I'm sorry," she said to Kym hurriedly. "I'll keep in touch with you. Can I get you on the *Leader* at any time?"

"Yes," said Kym, "ask for the City Desk."

She preceded him down the long, dim hall and paused before the sliding doors that gave access to another room. Pushing one door slightly, she smiled.

"Will you let yourself out?"

He bent his head in affirmation. She slid through the narrow space she had created for herself and as she did so Kym caught a glimpse of the room beyond.

"Well, I'll be damned!" he said as he opened the street door.

For he had seen, in the brief moment, a man with a short, light brown beard whose coat, burdened with a collar of heavy astrakhan, was thrown well back from his shoulders.

"Karl Meisterberg, huh? There can't be more than one nut in the world like that."

8
What Kym Discovered

He wasn't sure, after some forty-eight hours of earnest contemplation, that Mrs. Alton P. Bothwell hadn't made a fool of him. Certainly she had used him for her own purposes and it was purely a matter of chance whether those purposes would prove to be good or bad. He didn't intend to tell Dawn about it. Of that he was sure. In the first place, of course, he'd given his word to the woman in Chinese red. But when he faced himself with honesty he realized that the biggest motive behind his concealment of the facts from Dawn was the wish to keep from looking ridiculous in her eyes.

He could hear her, quite distinctly, telling him he had let a woman walk away with his wits. And he couldn't with any logic assure her that the woman, in spite of her air of mystery and her stubborn refusal to tell him what she was up to, had succeeded in convincing him that she was on the square. The thing didn't hold water and he knew it. He fingered, somewhat gingerly, the receipt to the safety deposit box in which he'd placed that morning the mysterious figure that had caused the professor's wife such agony of apprehension. It might get him in a lot of trouble before he was through with it and it might . . .

Slowly the strain of Dutch that gave his blue eyes their peculiar quality of clarity and determination penetrated to the surface of his consciousness. He set his jaw and made up his mind that since he'd started on the thing he'd stick it out whichever way it went. He'd trust, he felt, the Irish in him to pull him through with luck.

It was Monday. And since Kym had come to know Dawn Carson his Mondays hadn't been as blue as in the past. There was nothing, somehow, particularly conducive to a hangover in a day spent exploring the more deeply wooded sections of the Cook County forest preserves or in striding with a keen night wind blowing against your face along the hard-packed sand of that portion of the shores of Lake Michigan that extends northward between Waukegan and Zion City.

But even so there are Mondays and Mondays. And the Monday that followed the Saturday morning on which the body of Dr. Amos Cartwright was found in his offices was so unbelievably rosy that Kym found it difficult to credit his sense of time in regard to its existence.

They'd had good weather the day before—Dawn and he—on which to start for an all-day tramp. It had been one of those Sundays in late summer when the first hint of an autumn clarity had made the air like mild wine. Here and there, as they parked the flivver on the cinder road that led lakeward, a leaf drifted gently to the ground. They slung over their shoulders such light equipment as would see them through a single campfire meal with enough food left over to provide for supper on the homeward tramp.

They started off in high spirits, Kym singing loudly and more than a little off key as he swung down the wood path, dodged under a barbed-wire fence and jumped across a narrow stream. Once through the woods they took the track northward for perhaps a mile and then, just at the spot where a broken-down gate indicated only to initiates that the beginning of Blue Lupin Ridge had been reached, they entered the enchanted field that led to their Elysium.

Five miles of it, then, with swamp and quagmire on either side, rare stunted oaks, and pines twisted and dwarfed by long winters of harsh winds. And springing from the long grass in an ever-changing, nearly tropical profusion, a myriad of flowers. They emerged at last on a stretch of sandy beach at which point Lake Michigan took into its clear waters the sluggish stream that is known as Dead River.

Here they pitched camp, built their fire, made fragrant, muddy coffee, toasted bacon and snatched from the coals a dozen half-charred potatoes which they ate with full appreciation.

"Kym," said Dawn, after a silence of many minutes, "there's nothing in the world so good as this. Will we ever be old, do you suppose? Too old to love it outdoors with food that isn't, really, fit to eat, and sand blowing in our faces?"

Kym looked at her and then out across the water where a freighter, its long hull nearly submerged, was slowly disappearing toward the east. He took his pipe from his pocket, filled it thoughtfully, lit it and leaned forward so that his arms encircled his raised knees.

"Sure," he said, "sure, we'll grow old."

"And Kym," she continued eagerly, "I do love delphiniums."

"I thought we weren't going to talk about that mess today."

"I'm not—I only . . ."

"Well—since you've brought it up and can't blame me for it—I'd like to get rid of a thought or two that's been jogging around in my head."

"But I didn't bring it up. I only . . ."

"Ye-ah," said Kym, "but what I mean is: this murder's got more to it than shows on the surface."

"What do you know?" she asked quickly.

"Women," he observed, "always jump at conclusions. It isn't what I know but what I think."

"Oh! What you thi-ink!"

"Yep. Thinking's only looking at things and then letting them stew around in your brain a while. Well . . . Say, listen, Dawn, did it strike you there was anything funny about the way that guy, Cartwright, died?"

Dawn looked at him incredulously.

"It seems to me that everything was funny."

"Well . . . no . . . not if he died by poison or any other way that goes in a good, standard murder. Of course, there's always a lot of funny things but—well—there weren't any marks on him; there wasn't any sign of struggle and yet . . ."

He thought about it a while.

"He's got every other sign that goes with a regular strangulation case—eyes popping out, tongue protruding—congestion—suffocation."

He shook his head.

"I can't figure it."

"Don't try. This is a holiday. Let's keep it so."

They ran races along the beach, after that swam in the pleasant water and lay at full length on the wide, sandy shore. The sun beat down upon them. Toward evening when it had dropped behind the pines to westward, silhouetting the trees in a black decisiveness of outline, they gathered together the remains of their equipment, filled their pockets with chocolates and a few rough-made bacon sandwiches, and started southward.

They were returning home by the shore route that terminated ultimately in the cinder road on which their car was parked a mile or so west of the beach. Waukegan lay stretched ahead of them, a small, quiet city grown somnolent in the backwash of a departed navigation.

Dawn sang:

"Home along the windy sand;
    The dusk is keen and blue;
My eager fingers seek your hand . . .
    My heart leaps up to you."

She laughed a little nervously.

"Hm!" she said, "that 'to you' is a bit woodenish and the tune's all wrong, but . . . Lights are exciting in that place—just look at them, Kym, stretching out along the pier . . ."

"Where sky and water meet;
    The night wind sweeps against my face . . .
Exultant are my feet.

"Why is it," and she seized his long, obstinate fingers with her own that were infinitely small, quick and tenacious, "that the introduction of the word 'feet' invariably makes the sublime descend to the ridiculous with a plop? Now my feet are exultant. There's no other word to describe the way they feel right now—what with the hard sand, the necessity you're putting me to of forcing them to the utmost speed or which they are capable, the . . .

"Oh Kym! The slip is open!"

"Yes," said Kym, "so it is,"

They stood together, hand in hand, like two lost children looking down at the river that flowed so swiftly past their feet. The slip—of which this was the sudden, surprising outlet, was a thirty-foot channel that had been dredged from the sand by one of the big manufacturing companies that had so recently begun to build along the shore. Planned originally to harbor freighters it had been made both wide and deep and extended at right angles to the shore inland for a mile or more. But the project had fallen through and the slip had never been completed.

Boys used it for a swimming hole, frogs sang in the evenings along its banks, and a bar of sand, piled higher with
every inshore wind, effectually closed its mouth. But the
water had been quiet now for days past, and the slip, itself, filled to the brim by recent rains, had flowed across
the bar.

"It's not deep," said Kym meditatively.

"No," Dawn agreed, "but it's darned wet."

She sat down and began pulling off her shoes. Kym
made a sudden, wild resolve.

"Keep 'em on, Slim—I'll carry you across. How's that?"

She looked up at him and laughed. But when her gaze
encountered his she grew quickly grave and, leaning over,
tied the bows of her oxfords.

"All right," she said.

Kym thrust his big boots into her hands and swung her
suddenly from the ground. Her small, firm chin was near
his face; her dear, dark head rested against his shoulder;
and her light body, cradled between translucent sky and
turbulent water, was in his arms.

"Kym!" she said.

And while his feet still pushed through the rushing,
shallow stream toward the dry bank where he must put her
down he bent his head and kissed her.

It was this which, in the face of a five-eleven alarm, he
was considering on Monday. (He interviewed the Professor
on Saturday.) He sat on the roll-top desk in the City Hall
press room. The bell shrilled its staccato insistence that a
fire of importance and magnitude was raging in the Loop.
And McDevitt, his narrow head thrust through the door,
was shouting:

"Where's the fire?"

Kym's expression remained dazed.

"Where's the fire?" repeated McDevitt.

"Fire?" said Kym. "Fi-ire? What do you mean by fire?"

"Hell!" said McDevitt, and disappeared.

It was this—the fact that he'd gone instead of staying there like some new and increasingly irritating species of mosquito—that brought Kym to his senses. If McDevitt had gone like that instead of staying to fight it out something must be up. Oh, yes! A fire.

Kym reached for the misshapen piece of brown felt that he was impelled, for lack of other equipment, to call a hat, and slid out the door. But McDevitt was gone. The fact didn't bother Kym. Fires were not, strictly speaking, his meat, though he'd not, ordinarily, turn down a good one if it fell in his lap. He ambled gently down the hall in the direction of the stairs. Somebody'd be in the County Building press room.

"Kym," he said to himself, "hard-boiled Kymmerly getting goofy over having kissed a girl! And the girl's what they call hard-boiled, too."

He paused to consider that.

"But if anybody calls her that to ME . . . !" he suddenly announced to the lonely granite floor and the deserted corridors, "I'll knock 'em cold."

An elevator stopped in front of him and Fletcher's waddling, ill-kept body pushed itself between the partly-opened doors.

"Who'll you knock cold?" asked Fletcher.

Kym looked sheepish.

"Oh! Just a guy," he said.

"Say," said Fletcher, "seen the Carson kid around?"

"No!" said Kym.

"Well, I've got some dope for her. Say—you're kind of a friend of hers, ain't you?"

"Ye-ah," said Kym, "kind of."

"Well, and you're on the *Leader,* too?"

Kym refused to answer so obvious a question.

"I want to tell her something."

"I'll tell her," Kym said grimly. He looked down, now, at this fat specimen who had emerged from a County Building elevator only after going considerably out of his way, and whose connection with the Bureau had long been a source of wonder and surmise.

"Where you been?" he asked.

"Over at Cartwright's office with the Chief."

"And the Chief let you get away?"

"Sure!" said Fletcher. "The Chief's my Uncle Jim's favorite step-nephew."

"All right," said Kym, "what you got for Dawn?"

"Hm! Dawn, is it? Well—in that case . . . I'm not so sure . . ."

"Spit it out," said Kym.

"Well—why not be comfortable?"

Fletcher nodded in the direction of the County Building press room, the door of which stood slightly open.

Kym looked incredulous.

"In there?" he asked.

But Fletcher had already preceded him and pushed open the door that led into the bare, disorderly room where each succeeding quota of embryo journalists had thrashed out their theories, had revealed their faiths, and had watched the stuff that dreams are made of first grow evanescent and then vanish before the bitter actualities of soiled police reports. The room was empty.

Fletcher seated himself on the bare bench that ran along the wall and served interchangeably as desk and lounge to the men who used the room.

"We've found something," he said at last and in a voice that was intended to be impressive.

"Who's found it," asked Kym, "and where, and what's it all about?"

Fletcher regarded him with scorn.

"Just for being so damned smart," he said, eyeing the cigar that Kym had given him a moment before, "I'll answer the way you've asked. The Chief and me—we found it. We found it in a safe. And it's about the Cartwright case."

"All right," said Kym. "That's a good cigar, isn't it?"

Fletcher grinned.

"You see the Chief and me—we figured there'd be something in that safe that'd help us out. So I goes out and gets the combination from this Bothwell person—only one that seemed to have it—no relatives . . ."

"No relatives!" said Kym to himself. "At least she was honest about that."

"So this morning we opens it—and what do you think we find?"

On general principles Kym refused to look interested.

"A deed to the Thompson woman's property out on the North Branch."

"What about it?"

"Lord!" Fletcher exclaimed as though astonished at the Deity's laxity in allowing such stupidity to survive, "that just about sews her up. And you can tell Miss Carson," he said as he swung off the bench, "that she can go ahead with her story. The Chief gave it the release. Here's hoping she didn't get too sappy in her write-up, because there'll be a Coroner's jury that'll hold our Annie in its verdict this afternoon or I'm no detective."

Kym failed to comment on this. He was leaning forward and had picked up from the floor at Fletcher's feet a good-sized phial such as doctors use for holding supplies of drugs.

"Where'd you find this?" he asked.

Fletcher glanced at it indifferently.

"I picked it up on the floor beside the couch where the old guy was stretched out. It was empty. And it doesn't mean anything, anyway."

He ambled out the door.

Kym followed him and stood watching until he disappeared around the ell at the far end of the corridor. Then he ran back and seized an outside phone.

"Desplaines? That you, Holliday? Sa-ay this is Kymmerly. Let me talk to Emdig, will you?

"Emdig? Kymmerly. Listen—I want to get your opinion. No—no—personal—I won't use you without a go-ahead. Say, could a guy with heart-trouble get bumped off with an overdose of thyroid extract? Oh, don't be so damned conservative. What you mean is, he could. Huh? All right—thanks."

A moment later he had the desk.

"Elliot," he fairly shouted into the mouthpiece of a direct-line phone, "can you get hold of Dawn Carson for me and tell her to hot-foot it over to the County Building? Sure, we've got a story for you."

9

Feature Stuff

ANNIE THOMPSON TALKS!

And the scare-head was subtitled:

"*Leader* Gets Exclusive Interview with
Woman Held in Cartwright Case."

Elliot was exuberant. He let the story wind like an elusive snake through five pages of abruptly broken columns. He was sure as he had rarely been that reader interest would be carried easily over the repeated irritation of "continued on page six, column five." Because Dawn had struck gold. And since she worked it like an old prospector, he let her alone. She ignored standard methods; she consistently avoided stereotyped leads. She wrote:

"Geraniums! May the doctor's soul burn in Hell for them!"
  That gruff, harsh voice of Annie Thompson—and emitted, as it is, from between lips so narrow and austere. She is long, lean and sixty—this woman who is being held in connection with a death, and her face is an iron mask. Her brow is high and narrow and rises like a fortress above a pair of eyes that are keen as a hawk's. Gray, I think they are, and peer out above a nose that is thin, high and bent.

The scant flesh of her wrinkled face is stretched over the cheek-bones like leather—tanned with sun and wind—polished with age. She is of the earth with which she struggles for bread, of the elements that battle and defy her.

For at her birth Annie Thompson was sentenced to hard labor. The last—and therefore the least wanted—of a family of ten children, she shared in the eternal battle against poverty that could end only in one way—defeat. Her belated marriage was a brief, happy period of seven months when she was more than forty. And it came to a close, as all her hopes have done, in negation. A laborer, her husband was killed during a union strike. And two months later, in a back bedroom whose dirty windows looked out on scrap iron, and opened only to admit the clank and roar of passing elevated trains magnified to a crashing horror by the close, storm-permeated air of an August night, Sandy was born.

"Those were the days," she said grimly, "when Cartwright was as poor as me. Doctor? I don't know. There's some that said he wasn't no doctor. But he helped me bring Sandy here and that was enough for me. Yes—he helped with bringing him and then—then left him to die."

She'd counted a lot on Sandy. Her folks had early turned her loose to drift, and the short time she'd had with her man was all she'd ever known of love. So Sandy, she figured, would fill Jim's place, make up to her for all the work and trouble she'd had, and help make life better on ahead.

"It'd been hard enough going the last months after Jim died—what with no money and me able just to drag myself around. But I thought the child'd make it up to me."

"It's a boy," Amos Cartwright had said and then he'd left the room while Annie turned over to get a snatch of sleep. But she'd no more than dropped off when she heard the young one cry and she looked around. He was lying naked and unwashed on a heap of rags in the corner, and

even though the night was hot he'd begun, already, to turn
blue.

"Amos," she cried, "Dr. Cartwright!" with what little
strength she could summon in her voice. But nobody
answered. She managed, then, to pull herself to the edge
of the bed and so on to the floor. She dragged herself
across to where the baby was lying and covered him with
the sheet she'd clutched in her hand. Then, holding him
against her body to warm him she fell asleep.

"And when that man came in again he found us there,
on the floor. He was mad at me.

"'You'll kill yourself over a worthless brat!' he said."

And then, when she only pushed closer to the small
body that was beginning to warm by this time, he continued, "It's simple, Annie—a halfwit—and it may grow
up crippled, too, for all I know. It'll have a life of misery
and drag you with it. You'd best let it lie there. Nobody'll
know but you and me, and I'll be the last to tell."

Then he'd laughed.

"Maybe if he hadn't laughed, I'd have listened to him—
so help me, God—I was that distracted from being poor
and sick—that low in hope. But when he laughed, it
brought me to my senses.

"'He's mine!' I cried. 'I've suffered for him and I'll
work for him—and it's little you know about whether he'll
be simple or no. Such things are best left to God.'

"I've kept my word," she said, her eyes dropping to the
long, bony hands that had lain idle, now, for three days.
"I've worked for him. And they can't say he's simple," she
cried defiantly, "not simple. He's a bit different, perhaps,
a bit not like other boys. He wants more tending—more
love—but he'll give his heart like a foolish puppy for a
pat on the head. But," she paused, seemed to hesitate, and
finally announced triumphantly, "he's been a good lad to
work around the flowers!"

She'd taken to growing them partly by accident and partly from knowing it would help the boy to be outdoors. She kept her eye always on the lookout for a job where she could have him with her and, too, where he could be in the air. Bit by bit she worked toward the edge of town and only got her own piece of land when he was a boy half grown.

"Because Sandy was near on twelve when we bumped into Ike Watson one day on State Street. And that was the beginning. We'd come to look at store windows. It was Easter time—the Saturday before—and I hadn't a dime I could spare besides car-fare. There was twenty cents in my pocket and I'd promised Sandy we'd go in. I remember figuring then that after midsummer I'd not be able to take him on the car with me for half fare. He'd be twelve come August.

"We'd stopped in front of one of the big stores and Sandy was looking at wagons the way any boy will when I felt somebody touch me on the arm. I turned sharp, fearing a thief'd rob me of my back fare, and here it was Ike.

"I'd not seen Ike since a little after Sandy was born and I wasn't any too glad to see him then except that there were so few people I knew that a familiar face looked good—no matter whose it was. He'd grown up with me, too—Ike had—along with Amos Cartwright, and we talked over old days a bit as we walked along together. It was lunch time and he took us in and bought us a bowl of soup and a sandwich each."

That had touched her. For as it warmed her body that was shivering slightly as much from excitement as from the raw, spring winds, it reached her heart, too. It had been a long time since anybody'd been friendly—sociable. All the time they were eating, Watson kept watching the boy and at last he asked:

"What are you doing, Annie, by way of keeping yourself alive—you and the boy?"

She told him, then, about the job she'd finally got on the edge of town where, if she kept him quiet and always at the back part of the house, she could have him with her and out in the open.

"I'm aiming," she told Watson, "to get myself a bit of ground some day when I've saved enough—and raise flowers on it for the market. I know a lot about them from what I've picked up through helping the gardeners at places I've worked. It's what I've wanted most for some years now . . ."

"Tell you what, Annie," Watson said excitedly, "come back to the building with me and I'll take you up to see the doctor."

And when she seemed to recoil at the suggestion he assured her:

"He's a different man—been making money and more than ready to help out his friends. Why—he got me the job running the elevator in the building he's in, and pays me extra three nights a week for overtime. Maybe he'd see his way clear to fix things for you."

She went at that—reluctantly—and found the doctor not greatly changed except for a short beard he'd grown and the fact that he was dressed better than she'd ever seen him.

"But he had the same queer twist to his mouth—for all he'd been running in luck—the twist that made him look like he was laughing at a person."

"Hello," he said, his hand on her arm, "and is this the boy?"

"Yes, this is the boy." She looked at him proudly enough. He was as nice a looking boy as any you'd see— straight and clean—if a little on the thin side. But his eyes were bright.

"You see," she said, "he was worth saving."

"My mistake, Annie," and he laughed. "But tell me about yourselves."

So she told him all over again what she'd just told Watson only, in her extreme rectitude, hinting not at all at the hope that Watson had wakened in her heart. Apparently, however, there was some secret understanding between them or else Watson had managed to tell the doctor about it in the brief moment he'd spent in the inner room before they came out together to join Annie and the boy. At any rate he suggested, almost at once, that perhaps some sort of partnership could be arranged by which Annie could run the garden and he'd finance the deal.

"I'm a bit interested in flowers, myself, Annie—and perhaps a good thing could be made of it. I know you're honest."

At that he laughed again as though the idea, somehow, amused him.

"And in return," he went on, "perhaps you'd let me see what I can do to help the boy."

He went over and laid a hand on Sandy's shoulder and looked down at him with a kindly smile.

Her impulse was to reject the whole thing on such a basis and yet her good sense told her it would be best for all concerned. Perhaps the doctor could straighten Sandy out about his habit of following people he got to like—the few quirks that made him just a little different from other boys. She explained that Sandy was good, too good, and that his friendliness had, more than once, led him to follow strangers who had given him a kind word.

The doctor nodded, interjecting an occasional "I see" into her conversation. And when she had finished he talked to Sandy a while. Through his talk he won her confidence and when he suggested that she bring the boy up to him on Tuesday, Thursday and Saturday nights she agreed without question.

Gradually, during the course of her visits, the plan was worked out whereby she became part owner of two acres of land and a small house out on the north branch of the river. The doctor kept the deed with the understanding that she'd pay it off gradually as the garden began to bring profits and that, in case of his death, the whole property should revert to her.

He equipped her with plants and seeds, with fertilizers and tools, and he only asked as his share that he have what flowers he wanted and that he be allowed to visit the place as often as he cared to.

"Him and Sandy grew to be great friends—always puttering around together. And often the boy would take in some cut flowers or a potted plant when he went for his visits. Geraniums? Yes—that's what he took mostly. I guess the doctor had a special liking for them. Though I've never been able to figure out what he did with the ones he took. They always seemed to disappear somehow.

"It wasn't till here lately that I began to get nervous about the way those two hung together. Sandy, it seemed to me, hadn't changed with the doctor's treatments and he'd fastened himself on Amos the way he always did to somebody that was good to him. For a while past, now, a matter, maybe, of half a dozen months, he'd grown queer. Him and the doctor would look at each other and then at me—and they'd laugh. But it wasn't a mean laugh—more as if they had a secret about me they wanted to keep—a sort of surprise. I didn't pay much attention to them because things were going good and I was that happy—what with my work and a good living—that I didn't figure there was harm in anybody, along about then.

"I was a fool!"

Annie Thompson clenched her thin hands until the knuckles stood out sharply and when she raised her face from a contemplation of them its expression had changed. There was stark hatred in it.

"Friday—and I'm telling you, Miss, only because I've thought it over and I figure it'll be best for all concerned to have the truth. I'd not say a word to the nosey men as have been asking me about it. But you—you'll see the right of it and you'll put it in the paper so's they'll know it's true, won't you?

"Well—Friday, I went into town to do some marketing of sorts. I've always had Sandy with me wherever I went just to be on the safe side, and I'd got in the habit of leaving him at the doctor's office if I was to be gone long. I'd got the package of stuff for spraying my plants and I'd left it with Sandy while he sat down in the waiting room. That was along about four o'clock I remember because Sandy took his dollar watch out—it was new and he was kind of proud of it, I guess—to show me the time before I left. The doctor was busy in his office and so I didn't bother him. I'd done it often enough before to feel sure Sandy'd wait like a good boy till I got back. He always had . . .

"But this time he didn't! When I went to get him about six he wasn't there! And the doctor hadn't seen him. Or, anyway, that's what he said. And, of course, Ike Watson backed him up.

"'The boy's not here, Annie. And I doubt he's been here. You can see there's no sign of him. I've been in my office most of the afternoon, and I looked out just now when I heard the door open to let you in.'"

At that Annie lost her head. She pointed to the spray of flowers—delphinium belladonna—that Sandy had left, and seized the package of prepared lead. It broke as she dropped it roughly on the table and went pouring out over the carpet and floor. He looked rather frightened at sight of these evidences of Sandy's late presence, and tried to send Annie from the office.

"You'll have to walk down if you don't hurry. Watson goes off at six-thirty."

But she began to scold; her voice rose to a scream, and then she told him she'd have the police on him.

"Wild talk it was," she remembered sadly. "I was near crazy with worry. But I'd had the feeling growing on me lately that he was using the boy—turning him against me for some purposes of his own. I told him so."

At that he looked scared for a minute or two, and then his face turned hard—hard as rock.

"I've a visitor in there, Annie," he told her, "and I'd be obliged if you'd keep your mouth shut."

At that she looked across his shoulder to where the door of his office was a little open. She could just catch a glimpse of a big man who wore a beard—a light brown beard. And she remembered him particularly because, though it was August, he had on an overcoat with a fur collar—the short, curly kind of black fur that men sometimes wear. Then she paid no more attention to him because she was trying to get at the meat of what the doctor was saying.

"I've done no harm to him, Annie," he said. "But if he was listening, and I ever lay hands on him, I'll see he doesn't get back to where his tales will hurt me."

He seemed to consider a while and then continued:

"Annie, you'd best go home. You'll most likely find the lad waiting for you there. He's not so simple that he can't find his way home. Even a cat does that." He laughed—the mean laugh. "I'm going away tonight," he continued, "and I'll not be back. And, mind you, you're to let on to nobody until after I'm gone. But you've helped me more than you know, and I bear you no ill will. The deed to your place will be mailed to you tomorrow. You can grow flowers to the end of your days and there'll be none to stop you. Good luck." He turned to leave.

"But Sandy!" she cried. "What about Sandy?"

He looked at her and laughed again—and bowed from the waist like a foreigner—with his hand above his heart.

"Thank you, Annie," he said. "Thank you for the use of Sandy."

And as she quoted these last ironic, mystifying words, Annie Thompson dropped her head in her hands and wept. The walls that surrounded her were gray with city smoke, and the single window which shed light on her bowed head was barred.

"And then," I said, leaning forward to touch gently the scant knot of her hair, "what did you do then, Annie?"

She looked up at that, and through eyes that were rimmed and ugly with crying she gazed at me in wonder.

"Do?" she said. "What could I do? I ran out of there like a crazy thing—clattered down the seven flights of stairs to the street, and straight home as fast as. the cars would take me."

She paused, and all emotion slowly drained out of her face—even the bitterness and frustrated anger—leaving only desolation in its wake.

"Sandy wasn't there . . ." she said.

10

None to the Dealer

Still Monday—and a belated one o'clock. McDevitt of the *Post,* who had just come in from eating with a quick three-some at the Coffee Shop, was sitting on the floor of the City Hall press room with his thin legs crossed under him like a tailor.

The floor was dirty. So was the battered, roll-top desk that filled a good portion of one wall. So was the ancient table that leaned somewhat insecurely against the other and so, too, the three chairs that, badly crippled as they were, still managed to remain upright nearly half the time. The single window was both high and wide, but uncurtained, unshaded and encrusted with a month's accumulation of greasy soot, it opened on the dull, impatient grumble of the city. This subdued and steady metropolitan complaint rendered the sultry day hotter and still less endurable. The sun which, in open places, was doubtless warm with a golden light, took on as it penetrated veil after veil of acrid smoke, a brassy tinge.

McDevitt swore softly—and as if for solace.

From the big pigeon-hole in the desk the fire-repeater suddenly sent out a clamorous alarm that stung the heavy air like a swarm of angry bees.

McDevitt turned his head upon which the unruly hair stood out at eternal cross-purposes, and remarked indifferently:

"Five eleven—anybody going?"

Carmack's pale face which seemed to brood eternally over the sorrows of Erin remained passive, unaware. His enormous black eyes that stared owlishly but with incredible perception were fixed on the far corner back of the table in which direction, at intervals, he spat. Only his pointed chin, set like a weathervane to his degree of nervous tension, quivered slightly.

Hunter shrugged. He was lying, his head resting on a supporting hand, on the floor beside McDevitt. His scant, pale hair, brushed back from a deep forehead, his long, high-bridged nose, his narrow cat-green eyes that were arched with elevated brows, all contributed to an effect of insufferable superiority. Even his mouth, with lips deep-centered and tapering abruptly to thin corners, was scornful. Languidly he raised a half-smoked cigarette to his lips—drew at it delicately—and through the thin smoke of its exhalation only his eyes were intent, watchful, suspicious and alert.

"My God!" Kym shouted. "Why doesn't somebody say it? It'd do 'em good to spit it out."

He occupied the doorway, but in no conventional position. He was on his knees, his left elbow supporting his body, his legs thrust out in back of him where they crossed the sill with ease and extended comfortably into the corridor beyond. In his right hand he rattled a pair of dice, and, with no great preoccupation, occasionally threw them.

"Somebody'll get the fire," said Honnelly.

His legs that were both fat and brief were tucked under him, giving him the aspect of a contented Turk. But his round, rosy face was sullen. He wore a pink shirt, a lavender bow-tie, and on the back of his nearly bald, entirely glistening head, a derby.

"Which," said Kym, picking up his dice and dropping them into his pocket, "means that not one of us trusts the others two whoops in Hell."

McDevitt laughed wearily.

"Which means, as far as I'm concerned, that if this whole damned building started to burn down I'd wait till the fifth floor began to go—and slide with it."

"Ye-ah," said Kym, "that's all right to listen to, but I'll bet dollars to doughnuts that two o'clock sees five dead guys come to life with a whoozit. What-a-ya-say?"

"Sure," said Hennelly. "What's a fire?"

Kym stood up and brushed his knees.

"We've got fifty minutes to go. It'll be fifty minutes—more or less—before the heavy gentleman who is frequently referred to as the Coroner sees fit to release to a waiting world the sum total of the deliberations of such men as he employs to do his work for him. Plus," Kym's voice rose to combat a possible interruption, "plus that of the highly-esteemed citizenry who at present constitute his jury."

"He-ah!" Hunter called in an accent that was English by way of Australia.

But Carmack only spat again and said, "Shut up."

"Now my idea's this," began Kym.

"Won't somebody pay that guy," McDevitt asked the world at large, "to stop having ideas?"

"My idea's to be fair—no foolin'. You know I've got the longest legs, and the guy with the longest legs is bound to get the verdict first. And the guy that gets the verdict first makes the front page first."

"Honest?" McDevitt asked—spitting.

"I want to make this plain enough," Kym explained, "so that a bunch of soaks on the verge of sunstroke won't make any mistake about what I mean. We got to do something for fifty minutes or we'll go goofy. All right. Every last one of us thinks he knows all about who killed Amos Cartwright—and why. There isn't any fact to go on, but we've been filling in odd hours with figuring it out. Right?"

Hunter sat up and threw his cigarette into the cuspidor. McDevitt lifted his head from the floor, and Honnelly's expression of overfed disgust changed slowly to one of heavy curiosity. Only Carmack's contemplation of his own thin hands never wavered. His eyelids fluttered, his chin quivered slightly—he sighed.

"Let's deal for the verdict," said Kym.

"Huh?"

"What-a-ya-mean?"

"Right!" said Carmack.

"Here's the idea," Kym explained. "Each of us 'll pick on his own little pet theory—and think about it. We'll cut for the deal—ace high—five around and a no-limit draw. Stayers name their verdicts and the cards to show who's right. How's that?"

"Swell!"

"Rotten good idea."

"Why don't you patent that, Kym? Something for the children's Sunday?"

The draw gave Carmack the deal. He expectorated for the ultimate time.

Honnelly asked for one, though his defenseless face said he lied. Kym wanted two. Hunter shrugged, and called for four. Carmack gave three to McDevitt and none to himself. Kym stayed with him.

"Surprise verdict," Kym announced.

"The poison and the old lady," said Carmack.

Kym dropped his hand. The other four scrambled to get a view of it.

"Aces and kings," shouted Honnelly. "Show yourself, Carmack."

Slowly, and with triumph, the thin Irishman laid down three queens and a pair of jacks.

"And a pat hand!"

Kym took the cards.

"This time we'll deal for the scoop." A yell of protest greeted him.

"Not against your luck."

"Wheredayaget that stuff?"

Kym's expression was one of pained surprise. "I thought we had all that figured out. I'm giving all of you a chance to stack luck against my legs. If I get low I'll give way to the guy that gets high—see?"

"Good boy!"

"Large-hearted Kymmerly."

"It's the weather," said Carmack dryly.

Kym drew the deal. Carmack wanted one, and his sly, white face remained expressionless.

Hunter dropped out without a draw. Honnelly took two and McDevitt asked for three.

"And," said Kym, "none to the dealer."

This time McDevitt stayed with him and when he laid down four eights there was a roar through which the noise of another alarm could barely be heard. Then silence.

"The legs have it," said Kym, and put down, one after another, the ten, jack, queen, king and ace of hearts.

"It happens once in a life-time," Hunter groaned.

"And no stakes!"

"No stakes—Hell! A scoop!"

They played indifferently after that—anything to fill in time. Straight draw for a while, then dealer's choice with everything from seven-card stud to spit-in-the-ocean. Baseball brought the thing to an end three minutes before two with Carmack two dollars to the good on a two-cent limit game.

At ten minutes after the hour Kym dashed back over the sill of the room which he had left not long before. He knew that the other four would be held for a while in the County Building press room. Carmack would get the direct-line to the *American* immediately, of course—Hunter the *City Press* and McDevitt and Honnelly would try to kill each other over the first shot at the outside line.

Kym picked up the receiver of the City Hall phone and held his big hand over the mouthpiece so as to shut out the noise of a new alarm. Then he got his line and called his number.

"Elliot. Ye-ah. Hello, Elliot—Kymmerly. Do you want it direct or shall I give it to re-write? All right—here goes: no poison found in viscera—death due to natural causes— indications of heart failure. Nobody held. Now tie that up if you can. And say—Elliot—let me talk to Dawn Carson, will you? Ye-ah—that's all right—that's all right.

"Hello, Dawn. Kym. Just wanted to let you know that Annie Thompson'll be out among the what-you-may-call-ums again tomorrow.

"And listen. My hunch was right. Anderson's going to hook up the verdict with the dope about the thyroid. We're on the trail, kid—see you later."

11

The North Branch

The Cartwright story was dead. There wasn't a paper in Chicago that would use a line on it. For more than a week now Annie Thompson, her home, the country surrounding her garden, the tenements in which she had lived as a child, and the Desplaines Street police station had been photographed from a dozen different angles. Pictures had been reproduced of Sandy in infancy, Sandy as a boy of six, Sandy as a boy of ten, Sandy month before last. Analyses, both at first hand and by correspondence, had been achieved by professionals and amateurs; by psychiatrists, behaviorists, settlement workers, graphologists, students of astrology and Karma, ministers, doctors, lawyers, and by every citizen at his own breakfast table.

But even though her relations with the doctor had been gone into with minuteness and a courageous lack of reticence on the part of saffron-tinted journals, no trace of any sexual motive for the crime could be established.

Annie Thompson had been, in spite of the efforts of every big reporter in the city to prove that she hadn't, a tragically poor, remarkably honest and thoroughly hard-working woman. That the doctor's death had given her full title to the property on which she depended for shelter and food seemed of little enough importance when the fact was considered that he had never in any way interfered with her full use of that property previous to his death, and that he had exacted from her nothing in the way of payment save an occasional plant or a spray of cut flowers.

That the boy had been a factor seemed probable when she had admitted quarrelling with the doctor over his disappearance, but that Sandy failed to appear after a week of search on the part of private individuals and the police departments in many sections of the country proved at least that she had been honest in the matter. And when various householders, whose homes she had been obliged to pass in her frantic, hurried walk between the street car and her own isolated dwelling, agreed as to her presence in the vicinity at approximately the time she had stated, her alibi was well established.

Professor Bothwell's testimony demonstrated that she had not been in the doctor's office between seven-thirty and about half-past ten on the night of the alleged murder. And while there was no proof that she hadn't returned after that hour, there certainly was nothing to show that she had. Add to that the report of the Coroner's jury, and there really was no excuse for Hennery to hold her any longer.

But while he let her go with a certain amount of reluctance Kym was glad to see the old girl released if only for Dawn's sake, although he was inclined to agree with Hennery, for perhaps the first time in his life, that there was more to this accidental death than appeared on the surface.

It wasn't until he took his convictions to Elliot, however, that he realized how darned dead the story was.

"For the lova Mike!" Elliot exploded. "Get out of here with your theories. I'm sick of that story. It's a fizzle. There isn't even a good love element in it. If you want to

snoop around you've got my go-ahead, but if you run into
trouble with Hennery on account of it, don't come to me
to get you out. I'll use any story on it that's worth a column, but I'll be damned if I'm interested in a theory out
of gin by nicotine. Beat it."

Kym beat it—grinning. And went to Dawn. Dawn
might be a woman but she had some sense. And what's
more she was always willing to spend Sundays covering
miles of semi-wild countryside in any direction, and to
thresh out ideas over even the most meager of camp-fires.

The forest-preserve that wound along the banks of the
north branch of the Chicago River was practically bar-
ren of fire-wood. But what it lacked in that direction it
more than made up for in the way of paper. By Sunday
evening most of the foreign population of the northwest
section of the city had decided to return to their flats
for supper. And behind them was left a trail, a road, a
wide, horizon-sweeping Appian Way of paper. There were
newspapers, complete Sunday editions, wrapping papers
from meat markets and grocery stores, wax papers from
sandwiches and hard-boiled eggs; and boxes—shoe boxes,
stocking boxes, cracker boxes, candy boxes; and cardboard
cartons that had held matches, canned goods, macaroni,
cigarettes, Bermuda onions and jars of pickles.

Kym and Dawn usually arrived at the entrance of the
wooded tract shortly before dusk. This gave them time
and daylight in which to collect their fast-burning but
abundant fuel. They carried armfuls of it along the path
by the narrow, rapid stream, across two railroad tracks
and so into that part of the territory that began to spread
out into the plowed and planted fields of small farms and
truck gardens. Here for months preceding the death of
Amos Cartwright and when the existence of Annie Thompson would have been of no possible interest or importance

to them, they had rested on Sunday evenings beside an erratic fire that amused far more than it could possibly warm them.

On the Sunday evening immediately following their trip to Dead River, Kym and Dawn sat beside a fire that had burned to graying, windblown wisps, and neither of them gave a thought to replenishing it from the great pile of papers that lay beside them. Kym was working, by means of speech, on his theories about the Cartwright case. And Dawn, with not infrequent, often ironical observations was—she apparently thought—helping him.

"It's not only that," Kym was saying, "but it's the fact that, as usual, Hennery's gone at the thing wrong end to. How the devil does he expect to find out anything by digging up a lot of dope about a woman who's been out of this man's life for fourteen years? He'll find out more if he'll get at what the man's been doing with his own life during that time.

"Suppose he did give her a piece of land—free and clear. Isn't it the stuff to find out why he did it than why she took it? It's obvious to anybody but a congenital idiot that if a woman's poor and friendless and has a half-witted boy to bring up she'll grab at anything in the way of help—and without looking any too suspiciously into the motive behind the offer, either. But it isn't so obvious why a man like Cartwright should suddenly be seized with a charitable impulse of quite such magnitude toward a woman he hadn't seen for years and who meant nothing to him when he was seeing her. Get the idea?"

"Usual intelligence of perception," said Dawn with a twitch of her mouth.

"Ye-ah, well, here's the way the darned thing works out in my mind: Cartwright got some sort of scheme up his sleeve and he needed help in carrying it out. This Watson person—who's in with him or I'm a dumb-bell—joyously trotted Annie and the boy up the day he met them, and Cartwright saw his opportunity. He decided to use the boy—and quiet Annie's fears by giving her something to do in the meantime. Both ways—his supposed medical treatment of Sandy and his interest in Annie's garden—he cashed in on the opportunity of having Sandy where he could use him. Get me?"

She nodded.

"All right. Now a lot more happened on the night of Amos Cartwright's death than anybody's yet come out with. There was a row with Annie; there was a conference with the gent in the fur-collared coat; there was a séance; and there was the mysterious disappearance of Sandy. But there's stuff we don't know about in all that, and I'll bet it's nothing to what we don't know about the rest that happened on the seventh floor of the Umpire Building between four-thirty in the afternoon and midnight.

"There's one thing I'm willing to bet on, though, and that's that Amos Cartwright died as a result of hyperthyroidism aggravated by an overdose of thyroid extract. Elliot ran the story for all he could use, but Hennery won't follow it up. Says it's bosh. And there's not half the bosh in it that there is in some of the stuff he pulls.

"The story can be traced through five channels. And if we follow every stream we're bound to come, sooner or later, to a creek that runs to the river. There's Bothwell, Watson, the man I think's Karl Meisterberg (whom the police, by the way, are damned incurious about), Sandy and Annie Thompson—to say nothing of the Bothwell woman. Right now we've got everything that Bothwell sees fit to give us, and I think he's keeping something under. Watson's an idiot who's got just enough sense to save his own skin by keeping his mouth closed; Karl Meisterberg is incommunicado—and Bothwell pretends he's out of the picture anyway, though as to that I have my doubts. But that only leaves two available sources of information—Annie Thompson and Sandy."

"But, Kym," Dawn protested, "Annie Thompson's been pumped dry of everything she knows. And I don't think it's fair to bother her any more. Let the poor woman rest in peace. As for Sandy . . ."

"And there," shouted Kym triumphantly, "you have it. Sandy's the crux of the whole situation. Find Sandy and you find the beginning of the thread that'll unravel the whole thing. Find Sandy and you'll make Annie Thompson a happy woman instead of a creature that's going around wandering why an unjust God doesn't let her die and be done with it.

"Dawn!" he said, laying an eager hand on her arm, "we're not two miles from Annie Thompson's place right now. Let's hike over and talk to her—make her understand we want to help her find Sandy. She'll turn the place inside out for us."

He jumped to his feet and Dawn joined him. Together they started out at a swinging pace along the river path.

"Oh, Lord!" Kym suddenly exclaimed. "I've left my pipe."

He turned and ran with long strides back toward the nearly extinguished glow of their late fire. As he emerged from behind a broad-trunked oak he saw the slender, short figure of a boy, ragged and forlorn even in the faint light of the fire, dart suddenly back and disappear in the underbrush to the west. In his hand he'd held a half-eaten sandwich—a crust that Dawn had thrown away.

"Poor beggar," thought Kym, "wish he'd show up again. I'd give any kid as young as that four bits for a square meal."

12

Annie Thompson at Home

It was a small house—Annie's—low and earth-bound, painted white, and with green shutters. Dawn came upon it with her light, swift step that beat an interrupted accent to Kym's muffled, ambling stride. And she saw it for the first time just as the last few minutes of the evening's afterglow illumined and caressed it.

"Oh, Kym! She's got hollyhocks."

"Sure," said Kym, "what of it?"

"Kym!"

But she knew—or thought she knew—just what he saw: an ordinary little house with a disorderly appendage of outhouses straggling along to the rear of it; a rather makeshift hotbed, two cold-frames open now to the summer air, and an unpainted toolshed. He saw—she felt—an acre or so of land neatly cultivated, and planted in orderly rows of flowers that, under such conditions, looked little more exciting than so much corn; a white picket fence that enclosed both house and garden and inside the pickets where they ran near the house, a row of nodding hollyhocks.

But what Dawn saw was something quite different, and her heart cried out for Kym's acknowledgment of its existence. She saw a small, warm home set in its quiet and protecting grounds, encircled by a fence that had come

straight from the heart of a fairy tale. She saw peace and
happy work, the tools of home-making, and like a magic
barricade against worldly intrusion—material encroach-
ment—the tall and living symbols of perennial romance.

That Kym—as a man—had kissed her, meant less than
nothing—might even mean negation of any hope of love.
But that Kym—as Kym—had done so, meant something
else again. Because Kym wasn't like any man she'd ever
known. Yet he had refused so far, she was sure, to coordi-
nate the ideas of their mutual comradeship and the kiss.
Yes—Kym had a mind like that. It would take time . . .

"Men," she announced philosophically at last, "are
stupid."

He eyed her downward over the pipe.

"Meaning me?"

"Stupidest of the lot."

"Oh, I don't know . . . it takes brains to figure out a
really good killing. Now Hennery . . ."

"I wonder if his wife ever gets bored."

Dawn made the remark with such apparent irrelevance
that Kym took no trouble to answer it, but knocked, instead, at Annie Thompson's door.

It was opened almost at once as though the spare figure
in the gray calico dress ("I'd like to give her a pink one
just to see if she'd wear it," Dawn had once said) had been
standing immediately behind it.

She greeted them with what was, for her, a smile and
opened the door wide, inviting them to enter.

"If you'll excuse the looks of the place . . . I've not
done the straightening up I'd like. What with the back
work to catch up on—and Sandy's being gone. . . ." Her
voice grew husky—trailed off.

In the parlor to which the front door gave immediate
entrance an oil lamp was turned low on an oval table,
shedding its yellow light on a week-old copy of the *Leader*.

Two willow chairs with dull calico cushions flanked the
table; an enlarged picture of Sandy hung on one wall and a
chromo of The Rock of Ages—in scarlet and green plush—
faced it. The floor was covered with a bright, clean strip
of new linoleum. There was no provision for comfort, for
ease and relaxation—no couch or sofa—no softness in tex-
ture or line in any of the room's furnishings.

But through a door on the far side Dawn caught
a glimpse of the room that lay beyond. It was so much
brighter, gayer, altogether more livable, that she said
involuntarily:

"Oh, Annie! Do you mind if we go into the kitchen? It
looks so cheerful in there."

Annie hesitated.

"It's in a mess," she said. And then led the way.

On a small range where the fire was so low that its
radiance could barely be felt, a tea-kettle was humming
softly, and in front of the stove a gray cat, paws tucked
under, blinked indifferently at their entrance. There was a
splint-bottomed rocker, two straight chairs and a table—
the latter covered with a checked cloth and still holding
the remains of a meal that had, obviously, been served to
two people.

"I've had company," said Annie at last with the air of
a woman determined to lay all her cards on the table. She
stood facing them with her hands on her hips.

Kym raised his eyebrows but Dawn merely leaned forward and stroked the cat. Where Kym's attitude indicated
belligerent curiosity, hers was one of kind withdrawal.

"There's no good in him—I'll tell you that to begin
with," Annie announced after a brief, inward struggle, "or
he'd come out in the open and tell what he knows. But no!
All he wants is to find out things—and leave a body as
much in the dark as ever."

"Who?"

"Well," she hesitated, "I'll tell you. He tried to make me promise I'd not let on to a soul he'd been here. But I didn't promise. He can't say I broke my word."

"Who?" Kym asked patiently.

Dawn's look in his direction was nothing short of vicious. How would you—her glance asked—like to be old and somewhat poor, and bereft of your only son, and under suspicion of the police—and cross-questioned by a snip of a six-feet-two reporter?

He ignored her glance and waited for Annie to answer. When she didn't at once, he went on.

"Look here, Annie, I'm not trying to get something on you for the dicks. I'm no friend of theirs—believe me. But I'd like to get to the bottom of this thing—even though it's been dropped. Apparently dropped—because I don't think for a minute that Hennery's really let it go. He's just sitting back waiting for something to turn up—for something to give itself away so that he'll have an excuse for a go-ahead. And you know as well as I do that he's keeping an eye on you."

She was stoical—beyond fear.

"Yes," she admitted, "he'd like to send me up. I don't know why."

"No reason in particular—no grudge against you. But it's up to him to do something noisy once in a while just to keep on the good side of his support. And you'd be noisy. Get me?"

She nodded, but he knew that she hadn't an idea what it was all about. She was only conscious of her danger—and somewhat indifferent to it in the face of her loss.

"Now listen here, Annie, it would give me a good deal of personal pleasure to clear the thing up before Hennery does. And besides that, it would probably be the best possible thing that could happen to you. Because I don't think you're mixed up in it—and Hennery does. So if I follow my line—understand?—and dig up a story that hasn't anything to do with you, Hennery'll have to call his hounds off your trail.

"If you'll come clean with everything that's happened that I don't know about, it may go a long way toward helping me get to the bottom of the thing. And once we've reached the bottom," he paused, more effectively to accentuate the drama of his final selling point, "I have an idea we'll find Sandy!"

She stepped forward eagerly, and then her grim old face settled once more into its accustomed tragic lines.

"Yes," she said, "dead!"

"No," said Kym slowly, "I don't think Sandy's dead. More likely he's hiding some place—or being held."

"Who'd hold him?"

Kym shrugged his shoulders.

"It's just a hunch, I'll admit, yet it's got some sense behind it at that. I think that Cartwright was using Sandy and that the guy that bumped him off is keeping the boy under cover until things clear up. Sandy may know a lot— be dangerous . . ."

"Yes," she agreed, "and that's just why . . ."

"Annie," Kym interrupted with an air as casual as his excitement would let him assume, "did you ever lay eyes on this man who wears a fur collar on his coat—Meisterberg I think's his name?"

Annie's hand flew to her throat so involuntarily that Kym nearly laughed in her face. So he'd guessed right!

"Yes," she said, "it's him that's just been here."

"What for?"

"He was trying to get something out of me about Sandy—did I know where he was?—did I know whether . . ."

"Yes?"

"Mr. Kym—that man as much as said my Sandy's stole things—stole 'em for the doctor or from the doctor. I don't know which it was because I was too mad to listen."

"I wish you hadn't been," Kym interrupted, "we might have found out a good deal. Did he tell you where you could get hold of him—where he is staying? If he did, it's more than the dicks have been able to find out."

Annie Thompson at Home in "Yes. But I don't dare tell you, he'd kill me, sure, Mr. Kym."

Kym pushed his pipe between his teeth and thrust his hands in his pockets. He had been on the verge of telling her that people didn't commit murder as a regular thing, when he realized what a fool remark that would be under the circumstances. People not only did, and had very recently in the immediate circle of this woman's acquaintanceship, but the very man to whom she was referring might have done it himself.

The situation was difficult from all angles. Here he was—with some of the hidden facts of the Cartwright case almost within his grasp—stopped by Annie Thompson's fear of death. And a fear that was not unwarranted. Selected by fate, apparently, for the role of scapegoat in even the simplest of human contacts, she was doomed to walk a tight rope of diplomacy in order to keep intact the little that life had left her. He couldn't—with any justification to his own sense of right—use a form of threat that might force her to reveal the address of the man who held, obviously, important information. He'd run across, as a result of his impromptu call, a vein of luck. But the claim was staked so that he was unable to work it. He swore softly, gently, under his breath, oblivious for a moment or so of the two women who watched him—one with apprehension—the other with irony and love.

"Kym," said Dawn at last, "why not turn the tables on him? If Annie went to see him herself . . ."

He stood regarding her while the idea penetrated his worried brain, and developed rapidly under cultivation.

"Fine! That would put it over."

"Annie—will you do it?"

"What? See that man again? Not if I can help it, Mr. Kym. I tell you I'm afraid of him."

"But if it would lead up to finding Sandy . . ."

He let that notion take hold of her and work upon her frightened mind for several minutes. Then he continued quietly:

"You'd not need to let him know you'd talked to me. Just get at what's behind his wanting to find Sandy—tell him honestly why—that you want to find him yourself."

She nodded gloomily. The struggle between hope and fear was strong. Almost he had decided to drop the whole thing then and there, to let it drift toward its own solution or oblivion, when Dawn cut in.

"Annie," she said in that clear, crisp voice that carried conviction because it was always motivated by honesty, "Kym's mind's about half divided between really wanting to help you and very much wanting to dig up a big scoop for the *Leader*. Now I'm not in the scoop business. I'm used for trimmings after the scoop's been found, and I haven't an ax to grind when it comes to the Cartwright story. But I honestly do believe that it will be better for you—better for Sandy, perhaps, if things are cleared up. And I believe you think so, too."

"Yes, yes, Miss Dawn, I think you're honest—and good, too. And if I figured it would be any use . . ."

"Of course it would. That man's trying to hide—keep himself in the dark. And that shows, at least, that he knows something he's not keen to tell. Won't you help?"

The woman clicked her teeth tightly together, threw back her lean, melancholy head, and faced them both squarely.

"Yes—I'll do it."

During the next hour they outlined, minutely, her plan of action. How best she could approach the foreigner, how lead him to reveal his motives in seeking Sandy.

"How's he been getting by?" Kym asked. "I can't figure out why the dicks haven't caught him, seeing he's so free with traveling around to Bothwell's and your place. And any man who wears a fur collar on his coat in summer . . ."

Dawn put in quickly, "Don't forget, Kym, that Hennery never laid eyes on him."

"And he's not wearing the coat any longer," Annie supplied. "Though I must say he's not picked a very likely place to hide in."

Kym laughed. "You'll be telling us yet, Annie. Come on—it can't matter now. Give you my word of honor I'll never let him know!"

"He's at the Congress Hotel staying under the name of Karl Miller—and he dropped his coat over the Link Bridge a week ago."

A shout went up from two young and irresponsible throats.

"He couldn't have picked better unless he'd got a job in the City Hall," said Kym. "Trust 'em not to find what's under their noses.

"And you'll see him, Annie?"

Annie would—and what's more Annie'd like to show Mr. Kym and Miss Dawn around her place.

"It's a nice place—if the doctor did have his finger in it, and I'd like to show you the garden. That is, if there's any seeing to be done. It's dark out as seven black cats, and more than likely my lantern's out of oil."

She took it down from the hook on which it hung just outside the back door and, shaking it, decided that there was enough to see them through the next ten or fifteen minutes.

"Maybe, though, I'd better fill it . . . . ."

"Come on, Cautious," said Kym in a teasing voice, "let's take a chance for once. We'll not be more than a mile from the house if it does go out."

She lit it then and led the way toward the potting shed.

"It'll soon be time to start the fall work. And I've got to find Sandy before then or I'll be in a bad way."

She laughed, pretending to make a joke of his absence, as though it were voluntary and would, in all probability, be brief. The new note cheered Dawn; it was the first sign of hope she had yet encountered in this despondent woman whom she had grown to like.

"He was always good," Annie went on, "about dividing the irises, and taking up the dahlia roots. I plan to put in a lot of tulips and daffodils this fall for the spring market, and I'd counted on having him tend to all the potting. He's done the geraniums for near on two years—taken them in from the beds for winter forcing—and I was going to turn the others over to him this year—hyacinth and narcissus bulbs for Easter. Well . . ."

"Sandy took care of the geraniums, did he, from the start?" Kym asked quickly. "That means he had the potting of those he took to the doctor. Did you keep any sort of an eye on him or was he left to himself?"

"He didn't need watching—it wasn't much of a job once he'd got onto it and he seemed to take to it easy like. As for the doctor, I don't think he really cared what kind of plants he got just so's they'd be fresh every week. Anyway, he never made any complaint about it."

"Why fresh every week?" Kym persisted. "Sounds like eggs—did he eat 'em?"

"No—leastways I don't expect so. Fact is I was always too busy to give much thought to it. But now you bring it up . . ."

"Was he out here often, Annie—the doctor?"

"Pretty often—about once a week, I'd say. But he talked to Sandy and acted, sometimes, as if I was in the way. It didn't strike me funny for quite a while. I figured it was just extra nice of him to pay so much attention to the boy. There wasn't many that did. But toward the last. . . . And now he's gone. . . . I tell you, Mr. Kym, it all sort of hooks up together—see?"

"Yes, I see. And I see, too, how it hooks up with what the Meisterberg person said about Sandy's stealing. In fact," he paused, "it gets hooked up tighter and tighter with every fact that comes out. You go after the foreigner, Annie, and we'll clear the thing up yet."

They had progressed while they talked to a point directly in front of the farthest cold-frame and Kym, his eyes on the lantern which it seemed to him had begun to flicker ominously, failed to notice a small oak keg that stood directly in his path. As a result he ran into it. It tipped over, rolling along the ground for a foot or two before it stopped.

"Good grief! Where'd that thing come from?"

"It belongs in the shed," Annie explained with irritation. "And whoever's been snooping around here had best leave his hands off my property. If you'll just heave it this way, Mr. Kym, I'll see it's put back where it should go. I hope you're not hurt bad," she added as an afterthought.

He didn't reply for he was bending forward, examining eagerly the ground where the keg had stood.

"Swing the lantern this way a bit, Annie. I've found some loot."

"What is it, Kym?" Dawn, who had gone ahead, turned back at the sound of his voice.

"It's the cat!" Kym shouted. "The other jade green cat!"

"The other . . . the other . . . cat? Kym! Are you sure? How on earth. . . . And if this is the 'other' one, Kym, where's the first?"

"Rats!" thought Kym. "That's the devil of keeping things to yourself. They're bound to come out sooner or later—and then trouble breaks anyway. I wish I'd told her to begin with."

He stood up and faced her.

"Dawn, I'll tell you the whole racket on the way home. Meantime, I'd like to try and find out how this got here. Annie, did you ever see this before?"

"Yes, of course. I've seen a pair of such-like things in the doctor's office many's the time. But it's beyond me to figure how it got in my back yard. Unless—do you suppose the doctor left it here some time before he died? Do you suppose . . ."

But suddenly she, too, leaned forward and simultaneously with her cry of wonder and fear, the lantern flickered for the last time and went out—leaving them all in blackness.

But not entire blackness. For on the ground at their feet a circle of tiny figures glowed, phosphorescent in the still dark of the summer night. And it was toward this circlet that Annie stretched a shaking hand. When she stood up again and spoke it was in the voice of a woman who has seen a visitation—or a ghost.

"It's Sandy's watch! The one he took out to show me when I left him in Amos Cartwright's office more'n a week ago."

13

Amos Cartwright's Chemical Soul

Between them they had decided that it was time for the professor's wife to come out with her story. In fact, on thinking it over, Kym was fairly well convinced that it was Dawn who had decided it. However . . . he stirred uneasily in the comfortable depths of a damask-covered chair and wondered how long it would be before the lady showed up. The maid had said . . .

"Good afternoon."

The same voice, nearly the same words, and most of the same circumstances in which he had heard them on another day not very long ago startled him into equal dismay. He disliked particularly being crept up on—"stalked" was the word that came to mind—in a pair of heelless, soft-soled shoes. And it irritated him that he was disconcerted.

He had grown increasingly jumpy here lately anyway and it was partly with the idea of ridding himself of the chief cause that he had come to call on Mrs. Bothwell. It had been bad enough when one jade green cat composed or lead and mystery had been directly traceable to him through a safety deposit box, but now that the second member of the pair had come into his possession he was forever on edge with apprehension. He jumped every time Al Goodsol spoke to him, and he'd caught himself turning right-about-face when he'd confronted Hennery unexpectedly in the fourth floor corridor of the City Hall. There wasn't any reason, actually, why he should continue to bear the burden of those cats. If they were so all-fired important, they'd better be brought to light. And if they weren't, he didn't intend to go on making a fool of himself for any woman. But on the other hand it was instinctive with him to play square and besides, he felt that the Bothwell woman was honest. For this opinion Dawn had refrained, she told him, only by superhuman effort, from calling him a fool.

But fool or not, he'd come to lay his cards on the table. He intended to tell her that he'd run across the other cat and then put it up to her either to come through with the facts and so pave the way to revealing the whole affair of the cats to the proper authorities (Hennery included) or receive warning that he was going to do it himself—without the facts.

So that, as he had stirred uneasily in the depths of the damask-covered chair, he had felt that he was ready for anything. Anything—he now discovered—but Professor Bothwell's voice.

He jumped to his feet and his hat, which he had been holding on his knees, slid awkwardly to the floor. That made the situation infinitely worse because he was such a long way up in the air that to stoop over invariably detracted, from his dignity. When he rose now, his hat-brim between his fingers, he knew that his face was red. And this fact, in its turn, changed his aggressive attitude to one of apology. He swore.

"I hope you'll pardon me, Professor, I . . ."

"Ah yes, yes, of course, Mr. Kymmerly. I understand the situation perfectly."

("Which," thought Kym, "is more than I do.")

"I can comprehend your natural curiosity in a matter that relates so closely to the life or the late Dr. Cartwright.

Mrs. Bothwell is not at home, but as she has often dis-
cussed the matter with me and has indicated the possibility that you might, some day, return to pursue it further,
I am fully prepared to tell you all I know. Which, I assure
you," he added, rubbing his hands together and allowing
a slow smile to take possession of his sardonic face, "is a
good deal."

Kym was at sea. It had never occurred to him that the
woman who had made so desperate and secret a thing of
her concern about the cats had shared this secret with her
husband. For if she had, why was it necessary to make
Kym an accomplice? Why on earth couldn't her husband
have deposited the priceless piece of metal in his own box?
Unless—and here the intricacy and worry of his thoughts
rendered his mind a whirlpool of helplessness—the two
were in a conspiracy to involve him while going free themselves.

During this period of thought the professor's remarks
had been continuous but unimpressive, so that no word
of what he said had penetrated to Kym's consciousness.
But suddenly the tone changed from one of pedagogical
monotony to a strained vehemence that carried the words
harshly to Kym's reluctant ears.

"Death!" the weird little man was saying, his voice
raised in indignation, "death the all-powerful, death the
mysterious—bah! Decay! That's what it is—about as mysterious when it's looked at from an unbiased standpoint as
a can of garbage!

"You understand, of course," he continued, resum-
ing his normal dry manner of speech, "that this does not
express my sentiments at all. I am merely . . ."

("Then, why in hell," Kym wondered in a state of
exasperation, "tell me about it? What I want to know . . .")

"I am merely," the professor continued, "attempting to
give you some idea, not only of the mental outlook of my

late friend, but also an indication of his emotional pitch when once his—ah—what for want of a better term I am compelled to call 'spiritual concept' was challenged. Quite violent, I assure you—violent . . ."

"I hardly need tell you that we were constantly at loggerheads upon the matter. In fact it is probably just this marked diversity of opinion on a subject so close to both our hearts that brought us together.

"There is, I think you will agree, a touch of the reformer in most of us." He smiled indulgently. "And so of course Amos and I each felt it incumbent upon himself to change the ideas of the other."

Slowly—very slowly indeed—Kym was feeling ground beneath his feet in the strange waters in which he found himself. The professor was, he realized, launching into a dissertation on the conflicting opinions that had existed between himself and the late Dr. Cartwright—a conflict that had assumed such proportions as, ultimately, to find its logical outlet in print.

Cartwright's "Chemical Theory of Soul" had appeared almost simultaneously with Bothwell's "The Soul—a Logical Entity." And while neither pamphlet had caused much comment, save in University circles, at the time of publication, they had of course been brought to light and talked about at considerable length when the Cartwright story first broke.

"I can remember well," the professor was saying, "the first time I ever clashed with Amos. I had gone to his office on some errand or other and was brought to a standstill just as my hand reached the knob on his door. For a most unearthly series of sounds issued at that moment from within, and I assure you, Mr. Kymmerly, without shame, that I was struck quite cold with fear. I thought, I really thought, that some hideous death had just occurred.

"I waited, trembling, and the sound, instead of diminishing, increased to a series of piercing wails. It crossed my mind that help had better be summoned, and as I turned, in the greatest confusion, toward that rickety elevator, the cage passed and the man Watson—who still runs the thing, I believe—paused long enough to laugh at me. Yes! I assure you.

"'Go on in,' he said, 'there's nothing there as 'll hurt you. It's just some of the doctor's tricks—proving something for his own pleasurin'—he says.' And with that the man gave a pull on his rope and slid upward out of sight.

"I turned the knob and entered—still timorous to some extent—and discovered Amos bending over a tea-kettle which he had placed on the electric plate of his sterilizer. The kettle was steaming, and in its spout Amos had inserted a cork that was notched like a whistle. It was of course inevitable that a series of rather strange sounds should be produced, particularly when the cork was manipulated in such a manner as to graduate the amount of steam that was allowed to issue past the notches.

"The whole affair irritated me, Mr. Kymmerly, as being particularly arbitrary—a bit of child's play. And when he explained his demonstration as being one to prove that manifestations of so-called psychic phenomena were very easily imitated with the simplest of physical experiments, it did not alter my feeling. I could see no relation between non-survival of personality after death and the sort of noise that any small boy can make in springtime with a bit of willow twig. I said as much.

"This, of course, provided Cartwright with a splendid opportunity to launch out on his favorite topic. There were several other men present; a Ralph Long, whom I did not know; Ennis Cummings, whose theories in regard to interstellar vibrations were just then causing a good deal of comment; and the Bellotti, whose Latin chair at Northwestern had been growing increasingly insecure with such articles on Communism as had been appearing in the *Generator*. In addition to this he was an avowed spiritualist who insisted on giving demonstrations at any and all times. Altogether a contradictory character.

"'Furthermore,' Bellotti said as I finished my rather caustic comment, 'even you must admit, my good Doctor, that when a man has died something has gone out of him—something that was there a moment before is not there when he has, as we phrase it, passed on. Is that not so?'

"'What do you mean by gone out of him?' Cartwright snapped back. 'A rotten theological training in your youth has warped your judgment. That's what. You're a slave to a phrase. I'll grant you,' he continued somewhat more mildly, 'that each individual has a personality that is distinct from other personalities, and I'll grant you, too, that the personality ceases to manifest itself upon the death of the individual. But what does that prove? Nothing!'

"He bit the end of his pipe which, in his pacing of the room he had taken to smoking, and then, having bitten it, he swore at himself.

"'Cartwright's in a bad way,' Cummings murmured in my ear, 'he'll find himself on Mars one of these days wondering how he got there.'

"'When I die,' Cartwright continued, growing increasingly excited as he talked, 'I expect to go out—pff!—like that. And there'll be nothing left to show for it but a mass of chemicals that will, in time, form themselves into new combinations.

"'Personality! Individuality! Nothing more nor less than a difference in chemical quantities. Occasionally there is an absence—partial or entire—of some necessary element or group of elements. What have we? A criminal! A saint! A philanthropist, or a miser! Why you, Bothwell, you're a calm man because your thyroid secretion is insufficient; I'm a nervous one because I've got too much. While Bellotti there,' he laughed, 'I think Bellotti's liver is probably responsible for Bellotti's ghosts.'

"'Why,' he continued, 'what happens when a man dies? The processes of his body, due to some diminution in the supply of those chemicals which are necessary to life, have ceased to function because of the gradual inroads of decay—old age—disease. With this obvious chemical change which is known as death, the other, less easily discernible, more subtle change also takes place. The chemical and physical processes which heretofore, as by-products of the more obvious bodily chemical processes—mere emanations or reactions—have gone to make up the personality, have ceased to function also. With the cessation of circulation and the consequent lack of chemical distribution, the actions, reactions and inter-reactions that have previously manifested themselves as what the ignorant have termed the "soul," have likewise ceased to function. The plant's closed down. The chemicals are on the shelf.'

"'And do you really think, Doctor,' the undaunted Latin accents of Bellotti broke the spell, 'that this is the end?'

"'By all means—no!' The doctor's voice was a shout. He was always nervous like that—fearful, it occurred to me, that someone would present a better argument than his and prove to him in spite of himself that his restless ghost would yet survive him. There had been some foolish mention of a banshee at my dinner table one night and the sceptical doctor had turned as white as the damask of our cloth. I remembered then that, in spite of his essentially English name, he was more than half Irish.

"'Science is never wasteful,' he continued, 'never wasteful as mere theorists are. Nature never lets anything go wandering around in space, accomplishing nothing, serving no useful purpose.

"'I said that death renders the chemicals ready for the shelf. So it does. Just as a chemist returns to his bottles those quantities with which he no longer needs to work, so nature returns to her gigantic laboratory her chemicals— only she is more economical than the chemist—or perhaps only more wise—she wastes nothing.

"'Why, every breath you breathe throws into the air, among other things, carbon dioxide which is a rank poison to your body. But a plant in the room in which you are sitting or the tree under which you have sought shelter will take up the carbon dioxide which is necessary to its own life, but inimical to yours. You are living in that plant— and that plant in you.

"'Only, after death these chemical changes take place much more rapidly and more completely. You're used up— every bit of you—quite used up by nature—the great economist. There's transmigration of soul for you.'

"He laughed, pointing to a sickly-looking geranium that had tried its best to flaunt a scarlet bloom in the scientific barrenness of his office.

"'That is all very well, Doctor,' Bellotti said, his smooth voice losing none of its quiet certainty, 'but what I have seen, I have seen. If you will be so good as to be present at one of my séances,' his glance took in the rest of us, 'I think I will be able to show you some things that you cannot explain by means of chemistry.'

"We accepted his offer—the rest of us—and for a time met frequently at his house. But Cartwright never came. It was I, therefore, who introduced him to the demonstrations at which he so openly scoffed. In fact, as you have heard before, I believe, a séance preceded Amos Cartwright's death by only a few short hours. And he held his stubborn belief to the end. At least . . ." Professor Bothwell paused, looking quickly at Kym and as quickly away again, walked to the window and stood gazing out across the shaded lawn.

"Mr. Kymmerly," he said at last, turning, "I have hesitated to disclose my knowledge before, feeling that no good could come of it, and possibly that harm might strike some innocent person but, Mr. Kymmerly, I am convinced that Amos knew that he was going to die."

Kym, who had stretched his awkward length forward in the damask-covered chair, sat up suddenly.

"So-o-o?" he said. Then, "Do you mind," he asked his host, "moving your chair a bit to the south? The window back of you bothers my eyes."

He was not mistaken, he felt, that a momentary frown of irritation marked the professor's brow even while he changed his position and murmured a courteous "certainly." But whether that frown was over the insolence of the request or whether he found the new position disconcerting, Kym was not yet ready to say. At any rate the alteration in their respective positions had accomplished for Kym just what he had intended it should: it was now the professor's face that was illumined by the window and his own that was thrown into protecting shade.

14

What Happened at the Séance

The small man coughed, and placed the tips of his fingers together in a gesture that Kym had come to recognize as typical.

"Perhaps," he said at last, "I had better give you the whole story of that last evening."

He jerked his chair forward nervously.

"When I encountered on the Avenue the man whom I immediately accompanied to the doctor's office . . ."

"Do you mind," Kym interrupted quickly, "telling me his name?"

The professor hesitated, but only for a moment—a moment during which his expression changed so little that Kym could make nothing of it. He could only hazard the notion that hope, conflicting with fear, lay behind it.

("And," he assured himself, "you can't hang a man for that.")

"No-o, I can see no actual harm. His name is Meisterberg—Karl Meisterberg—and he came over from Rungaria, I am now convinced, on a secret mission. It was this mission that brought him to Amos Cartwright's office and it was in furtherance of this mission, I am sure, that Amos had planned to leave with him so abruptly.

"Mr. Kymmerly, I am going to ask you to do something for me. You are able, through channels of information that

119

are closed to those of us as are not involved in the dis-
semination of news through the public prints, to find out
certain things that it might be very difficult for me to
discover. Do you suppose," again he hesitated, "that you
could ascertain for me the present whereabouts of this
same Karl Meisterberg? And do you suppose—ahem!—that
you could gain any information concerning the present
condition of health of the King of Rungaria?"

Kym laughed.

"Rungaria? Is that a new kind of cheese?"

"No—no—a small kingdom in the neighborhood of
the Balkans—a new kingdom—quite a new kingdom.
And," he added quickly, "I don't want you for a moment
to attach too much importance to this request. Merely
a fancy of mine. However, should you happen to find it
convenient . . ."

Kym eyed him narrowly and decided, at once, to find
out all he could about Rungaria and Karl Meisterberg
(whose whereabouts he most certainly knew and about
whose movements and intentions he had already instituted
such inquiry as he thought wise). But he wasn't at all sure
that he'd pass the information on to the little professor
who had taken, now, to the nervous pacing of his library.

"When the news of Dr. Cartwright's intended departure reached my ears I was concerned for several reasons—
at least one of which I am not now at liberty to disclose to
you. But among others, I was disappointed to realize that
the séance which we had planned for that evening would
have to be postponed. I expressed myself on the subject.
At first Amos laughed at what he thought to be my too
great interest in a thing of such slight importance, but
after a certain amount of friendly banter he consented to
continue with our original plans.

"'My train won't be pulling out until 11:30,' he said,
'and we can go through with the thing—surely—before

then. And you know, Alton, you've not yet been able to convince me that there's anything in the game. You've never staged a real demonstration.'

"He turned to Meisterberg and explained the series of experiments which we had been conducting so far, I am forced to admit, without success.

"'Yes,' I interrupted, 'but I have an additional suggestion to put in operation tonight that I hope will bring results. Your sceptical attitude, alone, Amos, would be enough to drive away the most intrepid spirit. I am certain that if we create the right atmosphere we can induce at least one convincing spirit to visit us tonight.'

"At that I outlined to them the procedure which we later followed. Shortly after we entered that night I filled a bowl—the Chinese bowl which the police found broken on the floor of the outer room—with common table salt that I had brought for the purpose, and saturated it with denatured alcohol. This I placed in the center of the big table around which we had gathered, and at once turned out the lights.

"There was a startled gasp from Mrs. Bothwell as I struck a match and ignited the contents of the bowl. For immediately a ghastly flame sprang up and spread its light over every face in that black room. The flame was iridescent, blue to green, green to violet and back to blue again. We looked like ghosts and Cartwright's face was the worst of all. It was corpse-like, and his general manner like that of a man with palsy.

"For several minutes we sat quietly, the tips of our little fingers just touching. Nothing happened. I could see Cartwright's face, for he sat directly across from me, assume its normal aspect in as great a degree as it could with that weird light thrown upon it. Then slowly—almost imperceptibly at first—vibrations ran through the wood, and the table trembled slightly beneath our hands.

"Have you ever participated in a séance, Mr. Kymmerly? No? Then you have very little idea—I'll have to have you out here sometime. . . . At any rate the vibrations increased between Amos and myself. I could see his face clearly, and his expression was odd. I had known, of course, that the Irish in him would get the better of that cold brain once the thing had been accomplished.

"'Alton!' he called sharply, 'don't try to put anything over on me.'

"He was breathing quickly and his heart, dilated shockingly under the strain of years of hyperthyroidism, beat audibly in the subsequent silence of the room.

"The rocking motion increased until the table had succeeded in elevating the two legs farthest from me—this, I assure you, is quite the common procedure. When they were clear of the floor they dropped slowly again, tapped once, rose and dropped to tap again. As it lifted for the third time I began to give the alphabet, and the bowl of burning liquid, which had been sliding gradually toward me, dropped to the floor with a crash, extinguished itself almost at once, and we were left in total darkness.

"'A,' I said, 'B . . . C . . . D . . . E . . . F . . G . . . H . . .' and when I had reached the letter 'T' the legs abruptly touched the floor. The animating spirit of that table, Mr. Kymmerly, continued to possess it until two words had been spelled out. 'TRAITOR,' it cried, and 'THIEF.' I saw Amos rise, tremble, and start to leave the room. It was just at this moment—almost simultaneously with his gasp—that a series of four discordant crashes resounded from his inner office.

"We jumped to our feet at once, dropped the table, and I felt frantically for the switch that controlled the electric lights. Mrs. Bothwell must have preceded me in the dark for, when illumination had finally been achieved, she was in the doctor's inner office standing beside him while he searched frantically through his grip.

"The windows were broken as you found them; the pots of flowers were scattered over the floor, and the doctor bore on his face the look of a man who has suffered a great loss.

"'Anything missing?' I cried at once, for it was obvious that there had been an attempt at robbery.

"'No,' he answered, 'no—they didn't get a thing.'

"But his manner gave the lie to his words. He continued to gaze around the room in a distracted fashion. Suddenly he turned to me. His eyes were narrow and hateful.

"'You think you've got me,' he said. "Maybe you have. But all you can do to me is wipe me out. If I die tonight,' he rose from the floor where he had been kneeling beside his bag, 'there's a body of chemicals will turn and destroy you!'

"He gasped and clutched at his heart.

"Mr. Kymmerly, I knew Amos well—had long been acquainted with his malady—and I hurried now to help him. From his supply of small medicines I took a teaspoonful of aromatic spirits of ammonia, and while Mrs. Bothwell was administering this by mouth I prepared a hypodermic of dygalin and injected it in his arm. He recovered rapidly—with that buoyancy so characteristic of hyperthyroidism—and was quickly on his feet. But he avoided my eye and spoke sharply to Meisterberg.

"'We'll have to call a stop to this business,' he said, 'our train leaves in less than an hour.'

"Then apparently recalling the courtesy due from a host to his guests, he recovered a natural and friendly manner, and joined Meisterberg at the top of the steps. We said goodbye in the way that has been several times described to you, and left him standing with the foreigner beside him. I take it, however . . ."

"Professor Bothwell," Kym interrupted quickly, and as coolly as he could manage it, "are you sure of the contents of that hypodermic—the amount? Dygalin, I believe . . ."

For a moment the professor's face was blank, then it slowly turned crimson under the impetus of his indignation.

"Certainly," he said.

"All right, all right," said Kym easily, "but I happen to know the police and you, apparently, don't. If they ever get hold of that story you'd better not only be sure yourself, but have at least one good, unassailable witness who's just as sure as you are."

He swung to his feet, and as he did so the professor raised a commanding hand. "Wait! I understand, of course, your allusion, and I wish to let you know that my genuine reaction is one of gratitude. I was, of course, irritated and startled. I did not kill my friend, and it rather unnerves me to have it inferred. However—there's a question I'd like to ask you before you go."

He looked down at his nervous, twisting fingers, and up again at the tall reporter whose face, however shrewd and critical, could not be analyzed as being capable of anything bordering even remotely on the subtle or abstruse.

"Mr. Kymmerly," the professor asked at last, "did you ever—you or any of the men who examined the offices of my late friend immediately following his decease, happen to run across two cats—green metal cats? They were in the nature of book-ends, hollow, and painted a shade of green that made them, at a casual glance, resemble carved jade.

"They were very valuable to me—very valuable as—as mementoes of my friend."

Kym's face could not, it is true, easily express subtlety of feeling, but it could, with complete success, show infinite relief.

"Lord!" he said, reaching in his pocket and taking out the newspaper-wrapped object of so much inquiry, "take the damned thing—and tell your wife she'd better get the other before I lose my mind. And by the way, I intend to give Hennery the whole story tomorrow morning."

He expected to see surprise, gratitude perhaps, on the face of the quiet, small professor. But what he did see as he picked up his hat and swung out the wide doorway, was a man who, clutching in both hands a metal book-end, looked as though he had just reached the far, undreamed-of shore of his Utopia.

15

On a Mezzanine

The mezzanine of a Loop hotel, as Kym had long ago discovered, is God's best gift to reporters. To see without being seen, to hear without being observed, to wait without being either conspicuous or uncomfortable, what more can any man, engaged in the business of gathering news, ask of heaven than this?

Its chairs are soft, its carpet quieting to the self-conscious footfall, and its atmosphere—save in midsummer—rendered pleasantly warm and secret by the proximity of the ceiling. Here, too, at gratifying intervals, come such persons as are endowed with the qualities that go to the making of paper scandals: aldermen and bootleggers, gunmen and bankers, shoe-clerks and doctors, lawyers and merchants, sailors, detectives, actors, thieves and star reporters.

And here to meet them come their ladies: widows, grass and otherwise, wives and mothers, actresses, manicurists, ribbon clerks, usherettes, girl-friends, and the sob-sisters on noisy yellow journals.

Here then, after leaving behind him the swaying discomfort of an Evanston express, Kym sought the seclusion and opportunities of a chair overlooking the lobby. Like all reporters he was shy—shy particularly of being seen too publicly with the girl of whom he was proudest in the world. That girl, a Sunday feature still to write, had informed him in two sentences and a banged receiver that she would meet him at five sharp. The place he took for granted. And during the intervening hour he had his choice of the office, several police stations, two nearby press-rooms or the mezzanine where she would ultimately appear. Kym wanted to think, so he chose the mezzanine.

One by one he reviewed mentally the principals in this small drama of murder to which everyone, apparently, except himself and Dawn, had grown supremely indifferent. The chief reason for this indifference lay in the elimination of the word "homicide" which the Coroner's chemist had achieved by the simple process of an official report. He had not succeeded, however, in eliminating it from Kym's mind. For that mind clung tenaciously to the belief, supported by observation and deduction, that Amos Cartwright had died as the direct result of an overdose of thyroid extract, administered to a man already suffering from hypertrophy of the heart, induced by goiter. A silly notion, perhaps, practically an obsession, but one that had been supported as a possibility at any rate by one good physician and Doc Emdig. But the question was who—if his theory was correct—had had both reason and opportunity to administer it?

Sandy he counted out with very little thought. Sandy, it was true, had had frequent access to the doctor and had, in fact, borne some curious secret relation to him that had not, as yet, come to light. He did not believe, actually, that Annie herself knew what it was, though he felt quite sure that Hennery still suspected her. This secret fact, however, bore, he thought, more relation to that person or those persons who had actually caused the doctor's death than it did to Sandy himself. And, while he had never seen the boy, he was convinced that his mentality was such as to render him practically incapable of so involved a plan as was implied by Amos Cartwright's sudden farewell to life.

As for Annie, there were a dozen reasons for dismissing her as the possible murderer. In the first place she had not had a sufficient motive for such an act. The land of which she had become sole owner on Cartwright's death had been hers to all intents and purposes before he died, and while her early unfortunate experience at his hands after the birth of Sandy might have lodged in her heart a hatred that time and circumstances could not fully destroy—his later treatment of her had given her, certainly, no cause to bring that feeling to a violent climax. There was, of course, her openly expressed distrust of his later attitude toward Sandy; but even this, it seemed, had culminated in nothing more deadly than a noisy quarrel immediately following the boy's disappearance. It was possible, of course, that she had returned after finding Sandy not at home. But the fact that Meisterberg had been with the doctor when Bothwell and his wife had left made that somewhat improbable.

As for the professor and his highly decorative and (Kym was forced to add to himself) somewhat contradictory wife, there was, actually, no good reason to suspect them. The professor had the knowledge necessary to the perpetration of such a deed and, in spite of his avowed piety, was probably fairly free of inhibitions, but so far no reason for his having done it could be discovered. And the same facts successfully exonerated his wife. But there was something highly mysterious about that precious pair in relation to the jade green cats.

Why, since he had let himself become involved with them, hadn't he investigated their contents before? He kicked himself mentally and determined to go about discovering what was contained in those objects that, because

of their material, must be, despite their weight, hollow.
And he only waited for Dawn, and her cooperative interest, to carry out the plan. Until then the professor and his
wife must remain in a mental pigeon-hole marked: Suspended Judgment.

There were left of those whom he might suspect only
the man with the fur-collared coat—and Watson. Watson
he dismissed with something less than a serious thought
and concentrated on Karl Meisterberg. It was in pursuit
of Karl Meisterberg that Kym had sent Annie—in pursuit
of a man in whom the police had shown surprisingly little
interest. And the fact that Kym had seen him for a brief
moment in Alton Bothwell's highly respectable Victorian
front parlor only heightened his curiosity. At any rate it
was Karl Meisterberg who had last seen the late doctor,
and Karl Meisterberg who had, apparently, been closely
allied with him on a projected trip to Europe. The first leg
of this proposed journey was, in fact, to have started in
less than an hour after the professor and his wife left the
doctor's offices, and at that time there had been no plan
on the part of the foreigner to leave his companion.

Had he committed the murder and fled, taking with
him that for which he had come? But if this were so, would
he have remained in the city and country in which he had
perpetrated such a crime? And would he have at once visited the home of his late companions on the scene of it?
Unless—unless, of course, the three of them were involved.
It was possible, on the other hand, that he had killed the
doctor and then, failing to obtain that for which he had
done it, stayed in the hope that he would yet discover his
prize. Was not his visit to Annie an evidence of some such
probability? But what had been his object? Why had he
come in the first place? And what did he want? Of what
valuable thing could he have hoped to rob the man who
had planned to accompany him? The cats?

The cats! By the lord Harry—the cats! He refrained, only because he was civilized, from shouting the realization.

And it was at this moment that, out of the corner of his right eye, he caught a glimpse of two men rounding the corner of the mezzanine stairway. One of them was heavy and tall and dark, the other was heavier, short and of the sort of indeterminate coloring that is described on drivers' licenses as: eyes—hazel, hair—light brown.

Kym shifted his position slightly so that his back was turned more sharply in the direction of the stairway, elevated his copy of the *News* so as to conceal his face, and waited. In a manner at once leisurely and determined Hennery walked slowly the length of the mezzanine floor and sauntered back again.

"Here," Kym heard him say, "take this one, Fletcher, there's nothing left at the back."

Then the sliding of chairs over the padded quiet of the carpet, the sharp, brief contact of wood with plaster, an expressive exclamation.

He may, thereafter, have begun to talk at once, or he may have remained wholly quiet in somewhat lengthy contemplation of his thoughts. Kym could not tell. For from the lobby below a steady, subdued hum rose and fell. Occasionally the staccato note of a woman's shrill laugh lifted above the drone, or a man's voice, irritable and loud, made itself clearly heard. There was the constant shuffle and click of feet over the worn marble, the swish and bang of the big doors, both east and south, the high, monotonous, unintelligible wail of boys paging men whom, apparently they never found.

It was easy enough in such an atmosphere to think—once you'd got used to it. But it was very difficult, indeed, to hear. And for the life of him Kym couldn't tell whether Hennery and Fletcher were talking together or not. Then

suddenly a voice rose sharply—Hennery's voice—and
Fletcher grumbled a reply.

". . . Why didn't you nab him, then?"

"Nab him? What on?"

"Illegal possession—drunk and disorderly—resisting
an officer—Hell!—Fletcher—why should I . . ."

After that there was a mere jumble of words which Kym
didn't catch and about which he didn't give a rap. Then:

"Where's he now?"

"Back at the old joint—pulling the same rope as far
as I know. But I've got an eye on him. Mix any guy up
with the Cicero bunch and all you have to do is wait—if
you want him. Watson'll get his—and you know it. He's a
fence—sure."

"Fence!" Hennery's word was a snort. "If he didn't
bump him off, he knows damn well who did. And all I
gotta say is there was a swell piece of play-stuff pulled off
up there between him and the old lady. They fixed it—and
now they've got the boy where he can't open his mouth, or
I'm a dumb-bell. As for the stuff . . ."

Again their voices drifted off and Kym, for all he
strained his ears, couldn't catch another word. Watson—
huh? Well—maybe—maybe—but the truth of the matter
was that they wanted to stage a big conviction with Annie
Thompson, and they'd run onto a piece of luck. Watson!
Of course he'd tell any yarn to save his own dirty neck.

Kym glanced at his wrist—remembered that he hadn't
yet got his watch out of hock—decided it would do Dawn
good to wait for him, and swung quickly down to the lobby. Exchanging a nickel for a slug he ducked his head and
stepped into a booth.

"S-ay, Murphy—that you? This is Kymmerly—ye-ah.
Any news breakin'? No? Say—anything drifted your way
about a clean-up on the gang out at Cicero? No clean-up,
huh? And quiet—ye-ah, I'll keep it quiet—but did they

make any pick-ups? No—no—just got my eye on a story and somebody stepped on it. That's all—thanks."

He came slowly out of the booth and reached absently for his pipe, remembered that they'd probably throw him out—being a reporter—if he started smoking it and murmured,

"Hell!"

He ambled gently across the lobby, his blond head lifted above the crowd. It was true, then, there'd been a raid in Cicero—and Watson had been caught in with a bunch of gunmen and runners—drinking, anyway. He'd been let go—Fletcher's dumb-headedness—and Hennery was planning to tie him up to the Cartwright story. In that case it would break again and Kym's jaw was set that it wasn't going to break the way Hennery wanted it. When it broke it was going to break his way—and it was going to break right. In that event there was no time to be lost, he'd have to get going—and going fast—before tomorrow morning. The first step . . .

"Mr. Kymmerly!" A voice spoke breathlessly and a hand clutched at his arm. "Mr. Kymmerly, I'll call you at the office tomorrow morning at nine sharp. I must have your help. I . . ."

He looked down into the quick, dark, frightened eyes of Professor Bothwell's wife—saw those eyes glance apprehensively to right and left, and then she darted away from him toward the open door of a waiting elevator. As she slipped in, and just before the solid brass door closed with a soft click, another figure joined her, a figure that had appeared suddenly through the swinging doors that led into Clark Street—the figure of Karl Meisterberg, minus the fur-collared coat.

Kym stood, dazed and furious, gazing at the solid wall where, only a moment before, the man he wanted most in the world to see just then had stood for a fleeting moment. He knew it was useless to try to follow him. Another elevator, letting him out at a random floor, would get him nowhere. The two—Meisterberg and his accomplice, for that the word described her he was now firmly convinced—had hidden themselves as effectually as though they had dropped through the earth.

"Kym," said a small, humorous voice at his elbow, "Kym, dear, your mouth is open."

He looked down into the wise, laughing, willful eyes of Dawn Carson and closed it.

16
Interior of a Cat

At eight-thirty the next morning—an unholy hour—Kym
sat in the City Room of the *Leader* office before a desk
that he called his own because nobody else cared to claim
it. Once a respectable typewriter table with a drop head
and three fairly capacious drawers, it had reached the
stage of disintegration where the best that could be said
for it was that it still remained upright. Two of the drawers were gone and the third, holding odds and ends of
yellow onion-skin, fragments of erasers, several half-con-
sumed bags of cheap tobacco and a spare pipe, was minus
the upper half of its front partition. On the drop head,
now permanently nailed down so that its spring could not
leap to sudden and violent action under some unsuspected
cross-current of the stars, there rested what had once been
a typewriter. When Kym wrote copy for the desk—which
he seldom did—he borrowed Elliot's machine. While this
mangled remnant of a once-good instrument was retained
for his amusement when, under stress of a private idea, he
sometimes banged away, secure in the knowledge that the
missing vowels could not readily be supplied by the average curious passerby.

He was banging this morning—and looking glum—
when Elliot walked in.

"Great American Novel?"

"No!" said Kym.

"Follow-up to 'The Front Page'?"

"No!"

Elliot glanced over his shoulder. "Oh, I see, a cross-word puzzle bred to a mentality test. What will . . . say, Kymmerly, what's the matter? Got a hangover?"

"I don't drink," Kym explained with dignity.

There was a roar from the other end of the room where a group of reporters had gathered near the windows.

"Since when?"

"Since he met Carson."

Kym rose abruptly to his feet—his jaw thrust out.

"Shut up, eight or ten of you," he warned, "or I'll . . ."

"Better let him alone, boys," Elliot advised. "Kym's having a fit." Then he added in a lower tone, "When you snap out of it come over and get it off your chest."

Kym's belligerent expression softened. He glanced up at Elliot with a somewhat sheepish grin and, ripping the page of thin yellow paper out of his roller, he walked across to the City Editor's desk.

"All right," he said, "wouldn't that give you a head-ache?"

On the page that lay before him Elliot saw a diagram typed and with the vowels roughly penciled.

PRINCIPALS: A, B, C, D, E, F, G, X, and K.

"'A'," said Elliot shrewdly, "is, I take it, the corpse, 'X' the unknown, and 'K' the inquiring reporter. Right?"

"Right."

"But why 'X'? Haven't you got enough of a mess here without working on an unknown? And isn't one of these other members of the alphabet perhaps the unknown?"

"Sure," said Kym gloomily, "sure—that's just what I'm trying to prove."

Elliot dropped his head on his hand. "Oh, my God!" he said, and fell to studying the diagram again.

"A is well known to B, C, E, F and possibly to G—slightly known to D. Yet B, D, E, F, and G are kept in total ignorance of A's proposed journey with D. Upon discovery of it B is thrown into a panic, C disappears, E and F make plans to join A in a meeting that will take up most of the time immediately preceding A's departure with D, and G ostensibly goes home.

"Only—he doesn't. Actually G travels west at a rapid pace and joins several companions who are more often designated—in our better penal institutions—by numbers. His movements after the hour of nine, however, cannot be definitely traced. And it is somewhere in the neighborhood of ten o'clock and while A, D, E, and F are all busily engaged in a ridiculous dark-room demonstration of spiritualism, that X breaks into the adjoining room and apparently succeeds in stealing an object of much value from A's traveling bag.

"How do you know that?" Elliot snapped.

"Wait till you finish and I'll tell you."

Elliot read on.

"If X, then, is one of the principals, he must be either B, C, or G, because A, D, E, and F are all in the outer room when the robbery occurs. But B has the alibi of having been seen ten miles distant less than two hours previously and headed away from the scene of trouble, D has disappeared entirely and is, moreover, mentally deficient. Only G remains. And G, it later develops, is lined-up at a fence with a bunch of Cicero gunmen.

"A process of elimination, then, brings us to the conclusion that G and X are one and the same person.

"Which," Kym concluded aloud, "proves that it was Watson who stole the first jade-green cat, but I ask you, Elliot, but what the hell of it? That doesn't show who bumped off Amos Cartwright."

"Good Lord," Elliot fairly shouted, "I thought I told you . . ."

"Do you want Hennery to spring it then? Because if I don't, he will. And if he does the old lady's going to hang. He's got this Watson guy so sewed up, he'd swear pink was purple to save his dirty skin, and Watson . . ."

"Kymmerly," said Elliot at last, "do you mind telling me the truth, the whole truth and nothing but I ask you, Elliot, what the hell of it? That doesn't show who bumped off Amos Cartwright."

"All right," said Kym, settling himself comfortably on the edge of Elliot's desk, "you know it pretty well—minus a hole or two—up to the time that the Coroner's chemist made a corpse out of the story. One of the holes is the one I just filled in for you—about somebody's breaking into the doc's back room while the others were holding this fool séance, Cartwright's rush for his bag and Bothwell's statement to me that he was certain Cartwright missed something that was worth a lot even though he swore he hadn't. And to prove it, Cartwright passed out and was only brought to after a dose of digitalis administered by our friend, the professor."

Elliot's eyes were opening wider in a steadily increasing interest.

"Ye-ah," said Kym. "And here's where our little friend the inquiring reporter steps in to make a fool of himself." He swore softly. "Your friend Kymmerly," he continued, his voice tinged with irony, "drops around the next day with the bunch from the Bureau and discovers a harmless and somewhat idiotic looking jade-green cat in the bottom of the doc's bag. He shows it to Hennery who promptly appropriates it. The next day Kymmerly discovers it sitting cheerfully on the desk in the press room at Desplaines—tells the *City Press* boy what he thinks about

cubs—and walks off with it. Ye-ah," he said emphatically
in reply to Elliot's look of incredulity, "walks off with it.

"Then he ambles out to make a call on the professor,
bumps into the professor's good-looking and smartish wife
in whom he confides his possession of this choice and
funny thing, and immediately agrees—after she stages a
set or two of good old-fashioned hysterics—to buy himself
a safety-deposit box and plop the thing in there awaiting
her pleasure.

"All right, as time goes on he learns that the professor,
too, is interested in jade-green cats. But wait—on the day
previous to this discovery this same bright and shining
light of newspaper-dom ambles out to see Annie Thompson (curiosity, you know, Elliot, has killed more than
cats), finds out that the foreign gentleman with whom
Cartwright was supposed to make his getaway has likewise
been driven by curiosity—or some such motive—to call on
this same Annie Thompson. And his impelling motive—
aside from curiosity—seems to have been a pursuit of Annie Thompson's simple-minded boy in the belief that this
same Sandy was in cahoots with the doctor in a skin-game
of some sort.

"Kymmerly gets bright—and you've got to give Dawn
Carson some credit for keeping me from going completely
batty—and gets Annie to swear she'll look up the Meisterberg person and get some more dope out of him. After
which the three, Kymmerly, Carson and the Thompson
woman, start looking over the premises. As a result of
which Kymmerly stumbles—actually stumbles, Elliot—
over the second of the pair of jade-green cats which, somehow or other, has managed to get itself buried in Annie
Thompson's garden.

"All right. Kymmerly then goes out to Evanston for
the second time—no place for a reporter, anyway—and

encounters, instead of the professor's wife to whom he'd intended to turn over both cats as soon as possible (bright idea!) the professor himself, listens to a yarn with a lot of sum and little substance—and hands the cat over to the professor, telling the funny little guy to warn his wife that time's up on the other one.

"The professor throws more or less of a fit—gratitude or something, I should say—and the reporter leaves to take up his position on the mezzanine of one of our better known hotels. Here he hears the tale I've just told you about the Watson person—and from no less a character than Hennery himself supported by Fletcher and upheld by Murphy over at West, then encounters the female Bothwell in the lobby of the hotel, only to see her disappear in an elevator with Meisterberg—ye-ah—honest!

"But that's not the half of it, dearie," he continued, gloomily. "Dawn caught up with me about here and we went out to her apartment. I'd given her a release order on my safety box and she'd gone over and got the other cat out sometime during the day.

"Oh! My God! When I think that that girl went wandering around the streets for an hour or more—and probably laid the thing down in a wash-room some place . . ."

"Did she lose it?" asked Elliot quietly.

"No-o," groaned Kym, "but she might have—or been killed or something."

Elliot laughed.

"Get all your laughing out of your system now," said Kym, "because when I get through you're going to fire me, arrest me, and have me examined by a lunacy commission.

"Well, we got the darned thing down on the kitchen table and started after it with a hammer and the sort of a screwdriver that a girl's likely to have around a house. We couldn't budge it—or find any place where we could get an edge in. We made plenty of dents—the thing proved to be made of lead, all right, when we got going on it, soft and heavy, and then suddenly Dawn found a spring in one of the eyes—the same sort of simple arrangement that works a folding camera—and the bottom flopped out.

"Inside was the queerest looking rig you ever saw. There was a wooden semicircular block that held six small lead safes about four inches high. We took out one of the safes and opened it—something like a capsule. It held a yellow-ish powder that might have been anything from mustard to raw saffron."

"Good heavens, Kymmerly." Elliot's face was strained and drawn.

"Ye-ah," said Kymmerly wearily, "and even then we didn't fall. We put the thing together again and took it out to dinner with us!"

Elliot's groan was audible.

"After we got through eating we went over to Donneg-an's house—you know Donnegan, Elliot—chief chemist out at Seagrove and Bascomb—and asked him if he knew what it was.

"I thought he'd drop through the floor. Elliot—you know what it is—but do you know what the damn stuff's worth?"

"Not exactly," said Elliot faintly.

"All right. There are six safes in that case and each safe contains approximately one-half gram of radium sulphate and it's worth \$70,000 a gram! In other words the contents of that cat is valued at somewhere in the neighbor-hood of \$200,000—and I plopped the other one on the professor's desk yesterday afternoon. No wonder he looked goofy. Nice of me, wasn't it?"

"Kymmerly, where's the one you had analyzed?"

Kym waved a hand in the direction of his desk. "In my top drawer," he said.

Elliot jumped from his chair, walked rapidly across the room, flung open the drawer and extracted the cat from a nest of crumpled papers and old tobacco tins. Holding it somewhat gingerly he opened the office safe and deposited it.

"There," he said, "it can stay until I get Hennery over here with three of his men. He can probably get the other one from Bothwell without much trouble—pending an investigation—and," he glanced at Kym with commiseration, "as it's pretty evident you're as honest as you are dumb, I can probably keep you out of it."

The phone at his elbow rang.

"Here, Kym," he said wearily, "here's one of your women—and she sounds as though she was having a fit."

Kym talked—and listened for a minute or two—his voice subdued, his answers sharp and quick. When he finished he stood up and looked at Elliot with an expression of panic in his clear blue eyes.

"Elliot," he said, "if you can't keep that cat in the safe for another twenty-four hours while I do some of the fastest and hardest work I've ever done in my life, I'm done for."

He drew his hand across his brow on which the perspiration stood out in small, cold beads. His face was white and drawn.

"That was Mrs. Bothwell—yes, the professor's wife—the late professor's wife. Her husband was found dead on the floor of his study not an hour ago. And—yes—the cat is gone."

17

Amelia Bothwell

The prim maid who had opened the door to him on the occasions of his two previous visits to the home of Alton Bothwell acknowledged his appearance on the same threshold at ten o'clock by a nod, and the statement that he was Mr. Kymmerly.

He agreed, and she preceded him down the dark hall that led past the folding doors through which he had first caught a glimpse of the man with the fur-collared coat. Then, having arrived at the dark oak solidity of the library's sliding panels, she suddenly stepped back.

"Mrs. Bothwell—she's in there," she said, and slipped quietly around the corner and so out of sight. This was unprecedented and obviously the result of new orders. Always before she had opened the panels herself and, preceding him into the room, indicated a chair before she had left him. Disconcerted by the turn of events in a house where he was, after all, a stranger—and particularly in one which sudden and violent death had lately visited, he hesitated before the solid barrier of the doors.

"Mr. Kymmerly?" The tones were clear and cool—very distinct—and came from behind the panels.

"Yes," he answered in a voice as free from tremor as his situation would allow.

"Come in."

He fitted his fingers into the notches of the doors and pushed them apart.

She was sitting there curled up in a chair like a small, black cat and on the floor between them, as he entered, lay the body of her husband. He noticed with distaste that her manner was one of ease and while he shrank with a wholly normal male instinct of helplessness from all hysterical women he felt that hysteria would be better, more in keeping at any rate, with the present situation than the alien quality of this woman's eyes. Even her feet, tucked up beneath her brief skirt, were disdainful, and the hand that supported her resting head was raised casually on a graceful elbow. She nodded.

"You'd better look at him," she said. "I can't."

He looked. The body was lying face down on the rug at his feet, one arm crumpled beneath it, the other flung out stiffly. From the fractured skull a stream of blood had flowed to form a swiftly clotting pool, still red, but growing rapidly darker against the clear, soft colors of the Persian wool. A jagged cube of common terra cotta brick lay not two feet away, and through the shattered glass of one of the tall, Victorian windows that was unscreened, a summer breeze was blowing gently. The rug bore the distinct imprints of a pair of heavy shoes that had carried drying mud.

"Hm!" said Kym. "Not very much attempt to conceal ways and means. You've called the police . . ."

"Yes. Mr. Abeel will be here in a few minutes."

"Abeel—that's right—they've got a new chief out here now—haven't they? One of those imports from Detroit."

He stepped toward the phone which stood on the desk beside her.

"Mind if I use it? I'd better call the office. They'll want news, and I'd like to learn whether Hennery's coming on out, himself."

"Wait a minute," she cried and, seizing the phone, held it against her breast. "If Mr. Hennery is headed this way, there are a few points we'd better clear up between us."

"Time enough after I make my call. Elliot'll be expecting word and a delay looks bad."

"Listen to me," she said sharply. "I'm not a stupid woman; I'm not overly given to being driven by emotion or impulse. I'm not a woman to underrate the possibilities in any given situation. If I had been, I'd never have succeeded as Alton Bothwell's wife. As it is . . ." her voice caught, held for an almost imperceptible moment and then she made a queer and ugly grimace, "as it is I succeeded for two long years."

"If you don't give me that phone," Kym said slowly, "I'll leave. And if I leave, I'll call the office from the first public booth I get to. Too much time passed between your call to me and your call to the Evanston cops. I don't like it. But I can at least cinch my alibi if I call Elliot now. I'll help you any way I can—if there's any helping to be done. But I can't see that getting myself put in the hoosegow will keep you out.

"Fact is, I can't figure out why you got me into this mess in the first place—just why you picked on me. First you hand me a dumb-looking lead book-end and sell me—God knows how—on the idea of cadging it for you. Then—when your husband's murdered under damned funny circumstances—you call me up first shot and get me here before the police arrive. Meantime the second of the book-end cats has disappeared."

"An object which, you will remember," she interrupted quietly, and her tone was a distinct rebuke, "you happened to have had in your possession not later than yesterday afternoon. Where, by the way, is the first one now? Have you done something utterly mad with it?"

"It's safe—quite safe," he said. "Elliot's got it parked in the vault at the *Leader* office until Hennery gets around to picking it up.

"Fact is," he went on, his anger mounting as he talked, "I've taken too damned much on faith from you—and I've let myself in for a lot of trouble. Elliot'll do what he can for me, but there's a limit to what Hennery'll believe. It's God's truth of course, but who the hell's going to take my word for it that I didn't know I was renting a safety deposit box to hold a couple of hundred thousand dollars' worth of radium?

"Yes," he fairly shouted in answer to her frank look of amazement, "I've found out what you were letting me in for—and now you're trying to drag me along for the wind-up."

He indicated with an abrupt gesture the body on the floor.

Her face, which he realized had been white and worn for all its aspect of composure, suddenly flamed with a quick anger.

"Mr. Kymmerly," she said, "I was grateful for your help but you're mistaken when you imply that I 'let you in' for anything. This—this . . ." she, too, indicated the body, "has thrown me out on all my calculations. I'm at sea—and of course I realized that you were, thereby, at sea as well. There are a dozen intricate and twisted motives back of the very existence of the jade-green cats. And you and I—I am truly sorry that you are involved—have been drawn into the web that surrounds them."

She shrugged her shoulders.

"But because you have, I think it only fair to you—as well as to myself—that I tell you a few facts of which you are in ignorance before the police walk in on the crime.

"Oh, no!" she hurled out at him, "I'm not making you an accomplice to help me conceal my part or pervert the truth. I'm merely interested in giving you that truth so that you won't be trapped into a network of half-lies and contradictions.

"No, I'm not stupid, not stupid at all. And I realized at once, as soon as I saw Alton's body on the floor, that you would be involved whether I called you or not. Please realize and remember that, Mr. Kymmerly: *whether I called you or not.*"

He did—quite suddenly. His possession of one cat which, having been extracted from a safety deposit box of his own renting he had handed over to Elliot not ten minutes before Mrs. Bothwell's call telling him of the death of her husband, and his previous possession of the other, which he had turned over—with no witnesses—to the very man whose death had caused the call, were facts not conducive to a generous attitude on the part of Hennery. Hennery was anxious—for political reasons—to make it possible for the state's attorney to stage a spectacular conviction within the next few months. And, whether Hennery could actually manage to corner him in connection with a knowledge of the murder or not, the publicity attendant upon any suspicion would certainly not help him.

He saw, with a sudden terrifying clarity, how completely he was trapped as an accessory before the fact, if it should turn out that the woman had actually killed her husband; and he knew that his only hope lay in whatever revelation she might have it in her power to make. And as he realized it, he realized, too, that the body of the man whose death was rapidly engulfing him in a rising tide of danger, was still lying on the floor at his feet, and that the pool of blood had hardened and grown black.

"I'll have to call the office," he said wearily. "Give me the 'phone."

"All right," she said at last, and he took the instrument from a hand that no longer resisted him.

When he had talked with Elliot he hung up the receiver and stood drumming with his fingers on the edge of the desk.

"Hennery'll be here in five minutes or less—left headquarters right after I cleared the office."

"Mr. Kymmerly!" She was on her feet now—had taken a swift step toward him.

"Look out," he cried. "Your foot!"

But he was too late. Her shoe had already struck the soft, wet pool at the carpet's edge. She slipped, fell sideways, and as she did so her hand, outthrown to save her, encountered the dead man's broken skull.

"O-o-oh!"

A shuddering scream escaped the woman who had remained, throughout the discovery of death, throughout a conversation that had held elements of terror, wholly remote and poised. She sank slowly, gently, to the floor, her unconscious head falling back until it rested against the shattered one of Alton Bothwell.

It was in this manner, then, that Carlton Abeel—in uniform—with two of his men, came upon them. In this manner, too, that Hennery came clattering in a moment later. In this manner: with the unconscious body of Amelia Bothwell, held blood-stained and limp in John Kymmerly's arms.

18

Kymmerly vs. The Law

"Of all the damned young fools!"

Kym looked up, an expression of agonized virtue possessing his face. Before him stood Hennery, his hands in his pockets and in his eyes the glance of a father who has caught his small son smoking behind the barn.

"What the hell do you think you're doing? Galahad or Bill Dever?"

"Sorry, Mr. Hennery, but I'll have to take charge." Evanston's chief stepped forward. "I suppose," he said to Kym, "that you're the man Mrs. Bothwell mentioned when she called. Kymmerly, is it, of the *Leader?*"

"I'll say it's Kymmerly of the *Leader,*" roared Hennery, "and in about as tight a place as ever I've seen a young reporter. Now look here, my boy . . ."

"Sorry, Mr. Hennery," Evanston's chief repeated, "my jurisdiction—I'll have to cover the ground first. After that . . ." He waved an all-inclusive hand.

"All right. All right. But when you've got through covering it, maybe I can help you fill in some of the holes. Eh?" His shrewd, black eyes darted quickly between the reporter and the man in uniform. "I'm an old timer at this stuff, Abeel, and you're new on the job. I've heard you're a good man," he added by way of softening his previous bluntness, "but has it occurred to you that this thing hooks up straight to the Cartwright case?"

"Yes," Carlton Abeel answered slowly, "yes, Mr. Hennery, that's dawned on me, too."

"And now, Mr. Kymmerly," he said, "I'd suggest that you let one of my men take charge of the lady. The maid who let us in . . ." He stepped through the opened doors with a quick stride. "Come here, my dear, we'd like a bowl of water for your mistress—warm—fresh towels—and if you've any stimulant in the house . . . the Bourbon's safer, I should say."

She left quickly and Mr. Abeel entered the room again. His hands were clasped behind his back. Hennery sniffed.

"Mr. Kymmerly, will you tell us, please, what you know?"

Kym had been relieved of his burden by one of Carlton Abeel's neat attendants who had promptly placed her very much head down on the floor beside the body of her husband. And he was now occupied in using yesterday's handkerchief to wipe the blood from his hands. His face bore a grimace of disgust.

"Sure," he said, looking to see Abeel's noncommittal eyes regarding him expectantly and Hennery's frown of impatience and perplexity. "Sure, I'll tell you what I know."

He did, leaving out no detail, however incriminating. He began with the episode in the Desplaines street station when Al Goodsol had given him Bothwell's address, and he'd carried away the jade-green cat. He continued through his first interview with Bothwell, through the conversation with the professor's wife, and his subsequent renting of the box, through his discovery of the second cat in Annie Thompson's garden, and its brief possession by the man who now lay dead. He told, last of all, how Dawn had obtained the first of the cats for him from his safety deposit box on the previous day, how they had opened it in her kitchen and of the analysis of its contents by the friendly chemist. He told, then, how he had given it this morning to Elliot to whom he'd confided the story and of Amelia Bothwell's call following on the heels of this revelation.

"And so I came out here," he finished lamely.

"Yes! And so you came out here," Hennery grunted.

The maid had returned by this time and the same neat policeman who had lowered her to the floor washed Mrs. Bothwell's blood-stained hands and face with warm water and gently pressed to her lips a spoon filled with whiskey. The maid stood in the doorway, frightened and dumb. Her naturally dull countenance had grown blanker than ever with terror.

"Oh, sir," she kept saying, "oh, sir . . ."

Abeel informed her, "Professor Bothwell is dead, and the lady has fainted. You had better run along now and tell any other servants who may be in the house—and all the neighbors. Meantime I wish you'd stay where you can hear me if I call.

"She'll spread the story whether I tell her to or not," he remarked when her back had disappeared down the long corridor, "and I like to have things done on my authority when possible.

"Mr. Kymmerly," he asked, "under what conditions were you admitted to this house?"

Kym told him, including, as nearly as he could, the time at which he'd entered.

"Why didn't you call me when you left the *Leader?*" Hennery interrupted. "What'd you skip out here for and leave it to Elliot?"

"I thought it was Elliot's place. You've never been particularly cordial to newspaper information and," he paused, "I'm just a reporter."

"Why the hell didn't you call Evanston, then, as soon as you knew about it?"

"I took it for granted Mrs. Bothwell had done that."

Hennery's voice rumbled in his throat.

"You take too damned many things for granted. What's her story?"

Kym thrust his hands in his pockets and lowered his belligerent head.

"You'll have to get that from her. I'm no stool pigeon."

"Gentlemen! Gentlemen!" Carlton Abeel's half-humorous inflection commanded attention. "You're forcing me to repeat, Mr. Hennery, that I must finish my examination." He turned to Kym.

"Was the lady conscious when you came in?"

"Very!"

"You arrived here, I believe, at a little before ten, yet my office was not called until a few minutes previous to that time. Can you explain it?"

"I can only tell you," said Kym doggedly, "what she told me. And that's the fact that she wanted to talk to me before you came. She figured that I was involved—which any boob would recognize himself—and she thought she could help me out by putting me wise to what she knew."

"Why didn't you listen?"

"Because I knew I'd be in for just this sort of cross-examination over the time that had passed."

"Hm! Well—yes—but you have made it a little difficult, Mr. Kymmerly . . ."

"Sure," said Kym, "I wouldn't believe me, myself, if I was listening to this line of bull." He grinned.

Carlton Abeel looked at him sharply.

"And now, Mr. Kymmerly, how did you say that the first of the extremely valuable book-ends came into your possession?"

Kym hesitated—looked at Hennery—and away again. There was on the face of Chicago's chief of detectives none of that expression of combined guilt and consternation that Kym had expected to see. Either something was wrong somewhere or else Hennery was a bird of an actor. Somehow Kym couldn't believe the last.

"Al Goodsol," he said at last, "a *City News* reporter."

He noticed, then, that Hennery looked up quickly.

"And how, may I ask, did Al Goodsol get hold of it?"

"Yes," Hennery interrupted again, and belligerently, "where did Al Goodsol get hold of it—ignorant pup."

"I'm sorry," said Kym at last, "that you are forcing me to give it out, but you don't leave me much choice. Al Goodsol," he said, turning to Abeel, "got it from Mr. Hennery."

"You lying young whelp! You . . . Maybe I can't get you fired, but I can damned quick put you in the coop." Hennery's face was livid, his arms waving like those of a windmill with a good nor'easter behind the arms.

"Call me a liar again and I'll knock your face in for you." Kym's head was down, his hard, young fists doubled close to his body. "I'm reporting what I've been told. And I'll change it just this much: Goodsol told me he got it from you. He told me you brought Cartwright's bag up with you the day you trundled Annie over to the hospital at Desplaines, and that he took the cat out while you were standing there. He did not, it's true, say definitely that you handed it to him . . . but . . ."

"Then you'd better not say it. Be careful with your statements after this—and use a little of your newspaper anti-alibi stuff. When you're handing out a piece of information like that you'd better say 'it is alleged'—and say it good and loud.

"The last time I saw that cat was the day that Cartwright bumped off, and you hauled it out of his bag to show it to me. It didn't strike me, then, but it strikes me now mighty hard, that you were pretty all-fired interested in it at the time. I'm not fool enough to stand here and say you didn't put it back, but I can say—and without fear of being caught in a trap of my own making—that I never saw you do it."

"Gentlemen! Gentlemen! There is already one corpse in the room. And meantime it strikes me that the person to be questioned on this matter of Al Goodsol is—Al Goodsol. Am I right?"

"Yes, so long as you keep this young cockatoo where you can lay hands on him."

"I'm not slippery," Kym shot back.

"Oh . . . I . . . don't . . . know . . . about that." Hennery's eyes were narrowed now. "You were careful enough at any rate not to have anybody else around when you passed that couple of hundred thousand dollars' worth of cat over to the professor yesterday afternoon. How do I know, how does anybody know . . ."

"I hadn't an idea what was in it, then. I didn't know it was worth a small fortune."

"I suppose there's something in that. For if you'd known—then—you'd never have given it to Bothwell. But when you did find out you pretty quick hot-footed it back and . . ."

Hennery's temper, Kym saw at last was getting the better of his discretion and his sense. No use holding this line of chatter against him or getting hot about it, unless it grew dangerous.

Abeel cut in. "Careful, Mr. Hennery." He spoke softly. "Better resort to professional terminology. How about Mr. Kymmerly's 'it is alleged'?"

"What is alleged?"

The voice was very clear, if so low as to be scarcely audible, and of a feminine quality out of place in the rough and tumble of men's angry accusations. They had forgotten Amelia Bothwell, the three of them; had turned their backs on her and left her to the ministrations of the policeman who was bending over her now in the manner of a solicitous and slightly worried mother. The man from Evanston was the first to speak.

"Mrs. Bothwell, you know Mr. Hennery of Chicago, and Mr. Kymmerly as well, I believe."

"Yes," she said without hesitation, "I know them."

She had risen now and was supporting herself on an elbow. Her skin was pale. and the black hair drawn in ugly and helpless wisps across her brow where, water-drenched, it had dried. A faint streak of blood which the man had not succeeded in removing from her face trailed hideously across one cheek. Her chin, though, was firm and her dark glance unwavering and proud. She stood up, catching the desk for support, and let her eyes rest for a questioning moment on each of the men. There was no fear in them, only the slight hesitation of one who hopes that she will be believed. She walked slowly to a chair that was placed as far as possible from the ugly object that was on the floor, and sat facing what might possibly have been considered her group of guests. Her manner was perfect.

Kym noted that Hennery was obviously taken aback. He had, apparently, expected the woman to burst into a torrent of denial and accusation—to build at once a self-condemning structure of alibi.

Instead she concentrated her gaze on the face of Abeel and, smiling faintly, she said,

"Mr. Abeel, I have my story. I'll admit," she added, "that this turn in the plot throws me out somewhat but, properly analyzed, it will doubtless help to solve the whole thing and should, without question, lead us to the other cat.

"Perhaps," she said then, "I'd better tell the two men what it's all about. I tried my best to give Mr. Kymmerly some of the facts before you came because I thought it possible he'd stick his fool young head into a wholly avoidable noose—but that heavy fear of authority he's developed while working for the *Leader* wouldn't let him listen. And then I . . . the blood . . . I'm sorry . . ."

Abeel nodded. "Perfectly understandable. If you'd rather, I can sketch in the outline for Mr. Hennery. Perhaps you're still too weak."

"And deny a woman the right to dramatize her own story? Oh no!" Her tone was almost playful—certainly light of care. "If you knew how relieved . . . Really, Mr. Abeel, I've earned my bread during the last few weeks. Nothing, I am convinced, save a horror of physical violence kept me from doing that myself." Again she indicated the sprawling body on the floor.

"I'm sure of it," he agreed. "But you'd better go ahead. Hennery, here, is ready to arrest you right now for keeping him in suspense like this. The charge, doubtless, would be resisting an officer." He smiled. "Meantime, hadn't we better all go to a more—ah—pleasant room?"

She nodded and led the way through the opened doors. Abeel left his men in charge of the body with the ironic admonition not to disturb things.

"My only suggestion, Harvey," he said to the older of the two, "is that you don't add any more footmarks to the large collection that's on the floor. And I'd hint, further, that additional fingerprints won't help the telephone."

Mrs. Bothwell had already preceded them down the dark hallway, her step firm now, and self-assured. She pushed open the doors into what had doubtless once been called the parlor and stood aside while two men in uniform and another in a battered blue serge suit walked slowly in.

There was a marble, high-mantled fireplace upon which stood a pair of modern, wrought-iron candlesticks and a group of treasured silhouettes. There was an ancient carpet, rampant with pink roses on a ground of faded green and tan, two stiff walnut chairs upholstered in slippery black horsehair, and a sofa to match. The wallpaper was bottle-green embossed in whirligigs of gold; the draperies of brown velour, so heavy and dark that they succeeded in their apparent object of excluding from the nineteenth-century room they guarded such light as a violent Georgian age might have to offer.

From a stiff, walnut table that looked as though its feet were splayed, the lady in the thin black dress picked up a box of black wood mounted with a formal mat of *petit point*. She snapped it open and offered cigarettes to the three men, then lighting one herself, sat down.

"You see," she said, "if Alton had only stayed in here. . . . Can you imagine a murder being committed in this room?"

Hennery, Kym could see, disapproved violently of the cigarette and disapproved, too, of the woman who could refer so lightly to the death of her late husband. These two things, alone, would be enough to leave her open to suspicion in his mind. For Hennery's creed held that while a husband is always a husband a good cigarette is not a smoke—and particularly in the mouth of a respectable woman. Add to that the apparent understanding between herself and Chief Abeel and, as Hennery would doubt-less have phrased it, you had something. Kym watched the whole show with a curiosity and a suspended judgment that inclined him to favoring the woman. He couldn't help feeling that her story—particularly as it was partly, at least, known to the man who headed Evanston's police department—would have a tendency to release him from further connection with the murder of Alton Bothwell, and with the theft of the jade-green cats.

Hennery, he observed, was restless. It had probably occurred to him that the two men in the other room might walk off with the corpse while he was corralled in a stuffy room listening to a cock-and-bull story that was going to be pulled off by a good-looking woman of doubtful morals, who seemed to be in cahoots with Abeel of Evanston.

Hennery was not dumb by any means, not nearly so dumb, Kym admitted to himself, as he looked and acted. When once he'd got out from under the clouds of a stubborn determination to run the whole show, his mentality was keen enough, and granting that the woman had anything to tell that was worth listening to, Hennery's well-trained mind could deal promptly and efficiently with any action that it might be wise to take in consequence. Hennery was a bull-dozer who was too quick on the trigger of his temper, but aside from that . . . Kym didn't blame him much for getting out of order about the Al Goodsol yarn, if Al had put anything over on him. He wondered . . . Hennery's eyes had sought his, and a quick signal passed between the Chicago roughnecks who were penned up in a cage with two inhabitants of Chicago's high-hat suburb. Kym grinned and Hennery coughed before he looked away.

"But, no," Amelia Bothwell was saying, "I think that death, ultimately, would have caught up with him no matter where he'd hidden. You see," she faced them, "you see, Mr. Hennery, I'm afraid that what you'd call me is an accessory after the fact—the fact of Amos Cartwright's death."

19

Whom the Gods Would Destroy

"Dr. Cartwright was my employer—the first and only man I ever worked for. I had finished at Northwestern with an A.B. of which I was very proud, and had spent the four months following my graduation in learning stenography. But in spite of the conventional education, I had formed no very clear idea of what I wanted to do.

"I stayed around home for a while but money was scarce and I began to feel pressure from my father who thought I ought to be taking care of myself. He was probably right. At least I agreed with his attitude enough so that the Want Ad section in the *Leader*"—she made a little, mocking bow in Kym's direction—"became my light reading for a week or so.

"It wasn't the easiest thing in the world to get a job. As a stenographer I was absolutely green, and my formidable degree shrank remarkably when I exposed it in the cold air of business offices. Letters of application weren't answered and I began to think that all blind ads were deaf as well. I'd about decided to take up the offer of a publishing house to pay my fare to Appleton, Wisconsin, in return for learning a dozen pages or so of rigamarole, when I had a note from Dr. Cartwright.

"He explained—on a scrap of paper and in a disorderly scrawl—that he couldn't pay me much to begin with—

fifteen dollars a week in fact—but that my salary would increase if I proved useful to him.

"An interview convinced me that he was some kind of a bug, but I'd grown so used to that in a University atmosphere that it didn't bother me. The office was private and, from what I could see of it, informal in its management. I decided that I could probably work into a position of some authority and responsibility if I made the effort.

"I was right. In fact the time came when I wondered who, really, was the doctor in that office. Besides writing all his letters for him, running errands, receiving patients and keeping the place in some sort of order, I gradually became a half-trained nurse. He was so busy with what he pleased himself by calling his experiments that he had little time for anything else. He would make the diagnoses, and I would administer the treatments. In all cases, that is, save where radium was used. He was afraid, he told me, that I would be poisoned by contact with the mineral—and so he always handled it himself. I hadn't realized—then—that his supply of the precious and costly stuff was increasing out of all proportion to his need, and his buying power.

"I wasn't with him, of course, when Annie Thompson came back into his life and, after showing her a genuine generosity, he turned about and found so good a use for the half-witted boy he'd helped bring into the world. And I wasn't with him when Karl Meisterberg made his first visit, and conferred at great length with the man who then promised to accumulate a secret store of radium for his dying king.

"For by that time I'd married Alton. As Professor of Psychology at school he'd won my liking and admiration. He was older than I, and, of course, much wiser. He was respected and influential, and he came from a family whose

name was taken so completely for granted that the social
position it carried rested lightly—like a familiar garment
—on the shoulders of his self-assurance. So that his first
appearance in Dr. Cartwright's office came as a pleasant
surprise. I was glad to see him and he—so it seemed—was
equally glad to see me. His income, of course, was small,
but when he told me at the time he asked me to marry him
that his salary was all we would have to live on, it didn't
bother me in the least. In short," she laughed briefly, "I
am trying to tell you that I married for love.

"The fact that, like most things for which we strive
desperately, the love for which I married gradually dimin-
ished, faded, was eaten into by the incidents of our daily
lives, does not alter its original motive. I cared a great
deal for my husband until about six months ago—until
the change in him grew so marked that I couldn't ignore
it any longer.

"The fact of our limited income didn't bother him
any more than it did me—for a while. I'm sure of that.
We owned this home, and what entertaining we did was
among people who, like ourselves, derived their enjoy-
ment from gracious and simple living—mental stimulus.
Nicotine costs very little," she laughed again, "and we had
no special need of bootleggers. What liquor we kept in the
house was for emergencies and was not, somehow, looked
upon as a source of entertainment. If we had had wine in
our cellars we should have served it as a mannerly accom-
paniment to dinner, but since it had gone out of fashion,
we craved no substitute.

"I did my own work—all of it except the washing and
heavy cleaning—until a year ago. Then I took to coaching
a few pupils who were back in the subjects I had majored
in—and hired Dena. She's stupid, enough, God knows,
and lazy . . . but she looks all right answering the door,

and she can serve a meal properly if it comes, to a pinch. Besides—she was one of Dr. Cartwright's protégés, and by that time Alton had become soul-slave to his friend Amos.

"I have never been able to decide, often as I've tried, just what combination of influences started, and developed, the change in Alton. Instinctively religious as he was, with a religion, if you will, of his own making, the effect on him of close contact with a man whose whole philosophy was materialistic could only be destructive. He maintained, of course, up to the very last that he believed in the immortality of the soul—some sort of personal survival—but I have often wondered . . . felt that even his book was little more than the whistle of a small boy who finds himself suddenly alone in the dark. Cartwright's personality was pronounced, so much more vivid than my husband's. It could not fail to make its impression—and the séances . . . I think, perhaps, it was the pursuit of those uncanny manifestations which Alton was convinced were of his own initiative, that rendered him subject to the domination of Dr. Cartwright—the domination and, ultimately, the sinister rivalry between them."

She rose abruptly and walking across the room selected another cigarette—lit it—and returned to her seat on the low stool beside the empty fireplace.

"Mr. Hennery," she said, and her voice and eyes were directed toward that hardened official in a plea for understanding that had its immediate perceptible effect on his expression, "my husband changed, in a few short months, from being a kindly, generous, philosopher of life who took things much as he found them and laughed whenever they didn't go quite his way—changed to a bitter and avaricious thief. Yes," she said again, and the grim little smile played about her lips, "a thief, and finally a murderer.

"For that he murdered Amos Cartwright I am now as certain as though I had seen him thrust a knife into his heart. That the knife was a much more subtle instrument than the steel blade of any sword renders the idea, somehow, even more repugnant to me. I can understand swift, impulsive action—a murder committed in the heat of anger—even though I cannot imagine myself in that role of destruction. But my mind refuses to follow the mind of a man who could deliberately plan the death of his friend. And Alton . . . !

"Yet Alton and I—and one other—were the only people in possession of the information that would have been the cause for such a deed, and Alton the only man who knew of Dr. Cartwright's heart condition, of the actual, death-dealing quality of a heavy dose of thyroid extract to a man whose heart was dilated to nearly twice normal size and had a bad valvular leakage.

"Karl Meisterberg, of course, knew of the existence of the radium—had known of it since his first trip over here. But Karl would have no object, very little object at any rate, in stealing it. Karl, for one thing, is not a mercenary man. He is political by nature—a diplomat, fond of intrigue, but chiefly for its own sake. He had known the doctor, and Alton, too, for that matter, when they were all students for a short time in Vienna. Alton never liked him very well—considered him tricky, I believe, and when he heard that he had become involved in one of the sudden political changes that are always taking place in southeastern Europe he shrugged his shoulders and laughed about it.

"But that was before Karl's interest in his fly-by-night king brought him to America in search of radium. The king, it seems, and I can't for the life of me so much as remember his name, was dying of cancer. But the fact was being kept secret. It was, according to these dabblers in small-time politics, a matter of gravest importance that not a word of his serious illness be conveyed to other countries, and most of all to the opposing party within his own. Yet, since secrecy was vital, it was exceedingly difficult for Karl, who had been made Lord High Something-or-Other, to obtain radium in any quantity without arousing suspicion. Therefore the trip to America! And the peculiar destiny that, shapes our lives brought him, ultimately, to Chicago—still on a guarded search for radium.

"That was perhaps six months ago. I am convinced now that Alton had known of Dr. Cartwright's thefts for some time but it was not until after Karl Meisterberg's first visit that he realized what a stupendous thing the man was trying to put over. And when he did . . . well, money, it is said, is the root of all evil, and that applies equally to such commodities as, in compact form, represent great wealth. Four hundred thousand dollars is, of course, only a drop in the bucket of a fortune, but to men like Alton and Amos Cartwright who had lived simply enough all their lives, it represented a good deal.

"Alton discovered, and I was still sufficiently in his confidence for a while to have him tell me such things, that the doctor had been filching small amounts of radium from time to time from laboratories and the offices of doctors who were friends of his. At first it was done much as a pickpocket would gather silver—a grain here and another there dropped casually into a small lead safe that he carried always in his pocket. He had a few cancer patients, himself, was often low in funds, and the temptation first took possession of him under easy circumstances. Then, as he began to accumulate it, he began, also, to realize that these tiny thefts could be made to grow quickly into a fortune.

"When once it comes home to you that a grain of that precious, powdery stuff—a bit the size of a kernel of wheat—is worth somewhere near $5,000 I suppose it goes to your head. I don't know . . . but the problem of converting it into money had not, apparently, yet begun to bother him. I don't know how much he had gathered by this time—perhaps $50,000 worth. But the arrival of Karl Meisterberg and his coincidental revelation of his needs, given under a bond of secrecy that unfortunately for them included Alton, who was listening in the outer room, spurred Amos Cartwright on to a sudden and violent effort.

"He had been looking after Sandy for some time then, and his interest in the flowers was genuine enough. I have known a number of people—men especially—who were almost wholly anti-social in everything but their love of gardening. I wonder . . . But the boy's adoration of him— an adoration such as would naturally grow in the heart of a feeble-minded child for the man whose power had rendered his life, and that of the mother for whom he did have a deep affection, suddenly comfortable and good, proved too much for Amos in the face of his ambition.

"I began to suspect that Dr. Cartwright was using Sandy the first time I saw them together; for Sandy had the half-leering look of an imbecile who has been made to feel important. And yet I am hardly right in saying that Sandy is an imbecile—or was—for I don't know whether he's alive or not today; Sandy had a sort of wisdom that served him as instinct, serves a dumb animal. He was loyal to his mother—more loyal to her, I think, than the doctor realized. And nothing that came afterward could quite dislodge that loyalty. Sandy would do what he was told— following directions without judgment but with unerring accuracy—and when the doctor visited Annie's place out northwest and deposited his small lead cases in the pots of geraniums for such time as he thought it necessary to avert suspicion from himself., Sandy marked them well and never failed to bring the right pots into the office when he came on his visits.

"I didn't know, until I learned through officials of the Radium Society, from what sources he was getting his material. But one by one the names drifted in—the names of doctors—some of them in Chicago, some in Pittsburgh, Philadelphia, New York City, even in St. Paul and Minneapolis and Louisville, who reported that radium thefts had taken place in their offices. The amounts were often small—comparatively—a grain here and half a grain there, but in time the accumulation became large enough so that it looked like more than a coincidence of thefts. It looked like what it was: a systematized effort to corral a large amount of the mineral in order that it might be converted into money.

"It was only three months ago that Dr. Cartwright bought the jade-green cats. I know, for up to that time Alton told me all that went on. I wanted to report the thing immediately, but he urged me to be quiet until we were sure—as though the evidence were not before our eyes from the beginning. He bought the cats and made the wooden cases himself—Mr. Kymmerly knows how cleverly they were constructed—in such a manner that the rays would be permitted to converge.

"And Alton knew it—and I knew it. Yet I kept quiet until the afternoon on which Alton bumped into Karl Meisterberg hurrying to the doctor's office. When I learned of this sudden culmination of his plans, I insisted that Alton expose him at once—or warn him, at any rate, that he would be exposed before he could reach New York, if he did not abandon his plan to go East with Meisterberg.

"But I reckoned without Alton, you see. I had not realized—did not know—that Alton, who had stood on the side lines all the time, was determined, not to render justice as I supposed, but to barter secrecy for a share in the profits.

"And Amos Cartwright laughed at him. He was so sure that Alton could never prove any of his assertions, so sure that, once on European soil and with the money in his pockets he would get away, that he told Alton, in very simple language, to go to Hell."

She stopped and, stepping to the partly-opened doors, called to the maid:

"We'd like some tea, Dena—coffee for two of the gentlemen. If there are no cakes you'd better make a plate of cinnamon toast—a large plate, Dena."

"Instead of which," Kym observed, when she had rejoined them, "you strongly suspect that he sent Cartwright there instead."

Hennery frowned as became a man whose position requires him to register, invariably, the expected attitude, but the corners of Carlton Abeel's mouth, Kym noticed, twitched slightly as he lit his cigarette.

20

Right-About Face

She shrugged by way of commentary on Kym's judgment concerning Hell.

"That depends," she said, "on the form of your religious creed."

The small maid entered bearing a large tray. It held a pot of tea and one of coffee, and two square plates. On one there was a great pile of cinnamon toast, and on the other, doughnuts—crisp, brown doughnuts that were warm as well.

To Hennery and Kym who had been listening with an interest so intense that they had forgotten the passage of time, the food and the odor of hot coffee were like manna from heaven. It was, Kym discovered on looking at Hennery's watch which protruded from his coat sleeve on a bare, hairy wrist, nearly noon.

Mrs. Bothwell asked, "Where on earth did you get those, Dena?"

"Made 'em," said Dena without ceremony, "made 'em while you wait. Menfolks—they're always hungry—and cinnamon toast and suchlike truck don't fill 'em up like doughnuts."

A general laugh that was both spontaneous and light-hearted relieved the tension that had been growing in the group.

"That big fellow over there," she indicated Kym with a not-uncertain finger, "he'll hold lots."

"Very well, Dena—and thank you." Mrs. Bothwell's manner was suddenly dignified, her voice crisp and sure.

She poured coffee for Kym and Hennery—tea for Mr. Abeel—inquired about sugar, directed the placing of the walnut table so that it would hold the plates of edibles where they would be convenient for everybody. She was unhurried, confident, and serene.

Kym, watching her and considering these various facts, wondered again as to her self-control. How could a woman—any woman who was not a hardened and habitual criminal, a professional crook—take so lightly the death of her husband—no matter how abhorrent that husband might have been to her? How could a woman with her delicacy and charm discuss so quietly the recent incidents in her life with her husband, when his dead body lay stiffening on the carpet in a room not fifty feet away? He knew that he was simple, too simple, in his reactions and ideas for this world to which Amelia Bothwell belonged, and that simplicity forced him to cling to a feeling of repugnance—of distrust. He shook his head.

"What's bothering you, Mr. Kymmerly?" she asked, and there was a laugh in her voice. "Hell?"

He started nervously, so sudden and so acute had been her perceptive interruption of his thoughts, and turned—he could feel it—the blazing red that, in moments of embarrassment invariably swept over his blond skin. He nodded.

"As I said before," she continued, "your interpretation of whether Alton sent Amos Cartwright to Hell or not rests on the particular form of your creed. Just as my interpretation of whether he bestowed death on the body of his friend rests, primarily, on my later knowledge of the man I married. I have, of course, no proof that he committed the murder. But I have every reason to believe he did. He had the motive, the knowledge and the opportunity. And the change that had taken place in him during the last few months convinces me, now, that he was capable of having done it. Dr. Cartwright's appearance, too, as I have heard it described . . ."

"Yes," Kym interrupted quickly, glad of a chance to substantiate, outwardly as well as in his own mind, his previous support of this woman, "the *Leader* ran a story of mine expounding the thyroid theory more than a week ago. Perhaps . . ."

He turned to Hennery whose eyes were narrowed in a way that Dawn described as "the Sherlock Holmes disguise."

But Hennery continued to frown and only grumbled, "I should think you'd learned by now to keep your nose out of this business."

Carlton Abeel's controlled, evenly-modulated voice contributed, "Give him time, Mr. Hennery. Youth, you know . . ." And then to Mrs. Bothwell:

"And will you tell us now the rest of your story? I'm afraid the people at headquarters will be wondering if I've joined your husband in the Great Beyond."

Kym searched his pockets for his pipe, raised inquiring eyebrows to his hostess, and then settled into the consolation and comfort of a slow smoke.

"At any rate I think it must be fairly clear to all of you just what my action must have been when I learned of Amos Cartwright's death. I had asked Alton on our way home the night before what his conversation with his friend had been. And he assured me that the matter was settled—that Amos had agreed to call off the trip and to tell Karl Meisterberg that the radium was no longer on the market.

"You see," she explained wistfully, "I was still feminine enough in my desires to wish that the whole thing could be cleared up—justice achieved—without outward trouble. I felt that, if the doctor knew he was caught, he would be glad of an opportunity to restore the radium to its owners." She laughed shortly. "I had already created a mental picture of myself as the delivering angel to Dr. Cartwright, to the Radium Association and to the fellow professionals from whom he'd stolen it. I had a quiet plan all nicely outlined whereby I'd be the generous and noble go-between in the cause of justice—a justice without violence. No one with the exception of Alton was, so far, aware of my knowledge and my plans.

"And then Amos Cartwright was murdered!"

She paused, and the effect of the momentary cessation of her speech was to force the minds of her hearers back to the incidents—and the ideals—that she had just reviewed. Kym was stirred to a degree of admiration and of under-standing. And he could see that Hennery was affected, too.

"I know, of course, that the police have dispensed with the theory of murder in regard to the man, at least outwardly. But I am forced to use the term, whether Mr. Hennery accepts it or not, because of the incidents which followed its discovery. I was, as a matter of course, aston-ished, but I was appalled, too, by the sudden reversal of my plans. This death, I knew, would infinitely complicate matters. And when I confronted Alton with this fact he merely laughed at me.

"This laugh was the first hint I had of how things, as I am now convinced they were, stood. He told me rather abruptly that I had better mind my own business. And he informed me further that Amos Cartwright had told him to go to Hell.

"'Then why . . . ?' I asked, because I was once more at sea.

"'Why?' he sneered. 'Because he thought that he could cheat me out of my fair share of his loot. If you will remember, my dear,' he continued in a tone so greatly a burlesque of his former manner of love toward me that it froze me with fear and apprehension, 'Amos is not the only gentleman who has been traveling during the last six months. I have been to Minneapolis, myself—and Louisville, too, for that matter . . .'

"My expression must have shown, then, the horror that I began to feel as a realization of my husband's recent lecture tour slowly possessed my mind.

"'But Alton!' I cried, and he stopped me with a harsh grip of my arm.

"He was not a big man—Alton—but the passion for money that had taken hold of him recently had made him a brutal one. He thrust his face close to mine," she shivered at the memory, "and it was then that I began to be afraid of him.

"'You'll keep your mouth shut, my dear,' he said quietly, 'or you'll go the way he went.'

"Can you possibly imagine," she appealed to her audience, "how a woman with my background and training, my ignorance of any violence greater than the soft storm of romantic love, must have reacted to such a metamorphosis in her ideas concerning the man she had married?"

"Impossible!" Abeel murmured. "Impossible to conceive."

"I thought," the small woman continued, "that I was going mad, would go mad, with the sudden shifting of the ground under my feet. I had, in the brief space of two days, been forced to revolutionize my conception of life, of morals, and motives—of the attitude in keeping with a wife . . . .

"And it was very shortly after I had succeeded in deciding—in terror and with the hesitancy of a woman who finds herself for the first time confronted with the necessity of making a momentous choice—that I must follow my conscience and not my fear, that Mr. Kymmerly walked into Alton's study. And in less than ten minutes I discovered that he was carrying one of the jade green cats."

She paused, and Kym stirred uneasily in his chair. Was it possible that this woman—so clever with her tongue—would involve him, ultimately, so that he'd be unable to extricate himself? Dawn had been right. He didn't trust her.

"He told me then," she continued, "how, and from what source he had obtained it. And he had agreed to my hurriedly-conceived plan of renting a safe deposit box in his name. I didn't dare, you see, make any move that Alton would be able to trace. I didn't dare . . . !"

Kym breathed deeply. She had released him from suspicion as skillfully as she had drawn him in. And the mental reaction as far as Hennery was concerned would be more completely in his favor than if she had avoided such a trap. A darned clever woman—too clever . . .

°It was immediately after this that I went to call on Mr. Abeel."

Evanston's chief acknowledged the statement with a slight nod.

"I told him the whole story, from the beginning, including my suspicions, and I told him also that the other cat had disappeared, that two hundred thousand dollars worth of radium was in the hands of some person or persons unknown. I believe that is your phrase, is it not? And Mr. Abeel agreed with me on several counts: he agreed that we had no positive proof that Alton had killed Amos Cartwright and that secrecy in the matter would be our surest way of finding out; and he agreed that a silent and determined effort to locate the other cat would be effective where a police investigation accompanied by publicity would only serve to block our plans. And it was on this assurance that I went ahead.

"But last night my hand was forced." She hesitated a moment. "And this is the part of the story that Mr. Abeel does not know—the part that, I am afraid, is going to implicate me in the murder of my husband."

Her eyes were fixed unwaveringly on those of Hennery and once she had received a faint flicker of assurance, of confidence, from their depths, she turned to Carlton Abeel.

"I walked into my husband's study last night shortly after Mr. Kymmerly had left, and saw the second of the jade-green cats on Alton's desk. Mr. Kymmerly, he said, had left it. I knew it was the other cat because it was covered with a reddish clay, and I knew where there was an abundance of that clay. I know that Annie Thompson's delphiniums had failed at first because that very clay was a soil in which they could not thrive, a soil that needed lime and potash to sweeten it."

Kym started perceptibly, tipping the ashes from his pipe onto the floor.

"Yes," she said, "I knew you must have discovered it on Annie Thompson's property. I'm sorry . . ."

"I confronted Alton with the fact and he—he threatened me. He came so close to me that I could feel his breath—hot on my face—and he looked into my eyes with his own that were blazing.

"'If you lay so much as a finger on that cat,' he said very low but with an intensity that struck terror to my heart, 'I'll kill you before you can make another move.'"

She gasped audibly, and the sympathy of the entire company was wholly with her.

"I want to tell you—to assure you—that that is the last time I ever saw my husband alive. I left the room determined to get in touch with Mr. Abeel at once. I failed to get him at his office, tried to reach Mr. Kymmerly, and came back to bed. It was a horrible night . . ."

Kym glanced up quickly.

"And what were you doing in the Sherman lobby with Karl Meisterberg around five last evening? I'm not curious, only—you told me that you would call me at my office this morning at nine, sharp—why?"

Her eyelids flickered, and the first flash of anger he had ever seen her show illumined them for a moment.

"After I tried to get both of you," she looked quickly at the two men, ignoring Hennery, "I thought it best, of course, to let Karl Meisterberg know just what had happened—to tell him the whole story—so that he could make immediate plans for obtaining radium from another source. There are so many details—it can hardly be a cause of wonder that I should forget one of them."

Kym clung grimly to his point. "And how did you know where to reach him? The police . . ."

"You forget," she said with dignity, "that he had been a friend of my husband, and that Alton had been in touch with him from the beginning."

Kym nodded. A clever woman, certainly—a too-clever woman.

"And now that that's cleared up," she resumed her narrative, "I'd like you to follow clearly all the details of just what happened this morning. I forget . . . but . . ." she raised her eyes slowly. "Mr. Hennery," she said, "you'll have to believe me, and Mr. Abeel you must know that I am sincere. I'm placed in a dreadful position, the position of telling incriminating facts about a man who's been my friend. I am forced to tell you what happened—and leave you to form your own opinion as to the reasons.

"This morning I had breakfast alone at a little after seven—gave Dena my orders for the day, took care of the upstairs work as I usually do, and then—it must have been somewhere in the neighborhood of eight o'clock—I went for a short walk in the garden. I tended the roses, weeded the geranium bed, and came in to face Alton.

"I had seen no one in the garden." She said this last with marked emphasis, and then continued in a quieter tone, "I had determined to make my last stand for truth—

to tell him that I would expose him if he did not immediately give up the cat.

"He was dead!"

Her voice had sunk to a whisper now, and trembling as a woman who is forced to a terrible confession, she said:

"Less than five minutes later Mr. Kymmerly walked in."

Kym jumped to his feet.

"You liar—you double-crosser—you . . ."

He started across the room. But Carlton Abeel was in front of him. A whistle blew shrilly and the two men appeared immediately from the direction of the other room.

"Better give this man the cuffs," Evanston's chief indicated Kym, "he's threatening violence. And take him to the station. I'll follow . . ."

Kym knew the futility of resistance, but it took all the stubborn Dutch in his veins to keep the fighting Irish that filled the rest of him from striking out. The woman was sobbing hysterically now, curled up in her chair, and Abeel's fine face bore a look of worry and misgiving—or so Kym thought. Only Hennery registered nothing, standing with his short, heavy legs balanced wide apart, his hands thrust deep in his pockets, and his bulldog jaw thrust forward. He was looking at Kym.

"Kid," he said at last, "I can't countermand an order in this man's territory, but I have Elliot's word for it that you answered the woman's call in the office at around eight-forty-five. Besides which, though you may be a damned young fool, you're no murderer, and you're no liar." He paused. Finally he shot out:

"What's the Carson kid's name—Dawn? All right—you sit tight—she'd interview the devil himself to save you. Between us we'll see you through."

He turned his back on the room and all its occupants, and walked rapidly out between the folding black walnut doors.

21

John Kymmerly

Experience, he decided as he walked between the two men in uniform and entered the waiting patrol, had its advantages. If he hadn't seen so many poor bums trying to fight the cops when they were arrested, he'd have made a bull-headed Irish attempt to clean 'em up and get away. But he knew better. He knew that a policy of watchful waiting was composed of something besides hot air, and that a man who was as well known and as conspicuous in the Chicago police and newspaper world as John Kymmerly wouldn't have a rabbit's chance if he tried to break.

Hennery might be for him now—God most emphatically bless him—but Hennery belonged to Chicago and had no jurisdiction in the Evanston police department. Hennery might be able to prove—would be able to prove by means of Elliot's testimony—a perfect alibi for him. But until Hennery succeeded in getting into gear the somewhat cumbersome machinery of the law, he'd have to sit tight. And in the meantime he'd save himself trouble and a certain amount of superfluous bodily injury by accepting, with what grace he could muster, his present predicament.

Elliot's word was as good as gold—as good as platinum—as good, in fact (and he laughed at the thought) as four or five grams of radium contained in a couple of jade-green cats. And Elliot—plus Kline who did the theaters—

plus Effingwell who ran the column—plus several police reporters who had happened to be in the city room at a quarter of nine that morning, could all testify very freely that Kymmerly had been there, too. And Elliot could testify further that Kym had told him of Professor Bothwell's death as it had been reported by his wife over the phone, at a time remarkably coincident with her avowed reception of him at the house. To say nothing of the maid who had let him in at nearly ten o'clock.

Why the woman was a fool! What did she expect to accomplish by throwing the blame on him when common sense would have told her that her statement would be given the lie before twenty-four hours had passed? Maybe she thought he was of no account—only an everyday reporter with the cards stacked against him. But if that was her line she hadn't thought far enough—because, while as an individual he didn't matter a straw to Chicago, to its police department or very greatly to its newspapers, as a member of the *Leader* staff he mattered a lot. The *Leader,* to save its own face, would start from the inside out and get the police doing double duty to exonerate one of its reporters. And the *Leader* was a power in the city not to be underestimated.

Twenty-four hours—that would be the outermost limit on the time she'd gain. And after that they'd start on her—the whole pack of hounds that ran the public press of Chicago. Twenty-four hours—maybe less—twenty-four hours—hm! . . . twenty-four hours . . .

Good Lord! That's all she wanted—all she'd need—to clear the city—to clear the country even . . . A smart woman that—a damned smart woman. He began to look around him with more hope in his heart than he'd felt since yesterday. Twenty-four hours! Yes—that was it. Meantime he'd probably spend the night in the Evanston hoosegow; and if it was as good as the thing he was riding in he'd have no particular kick to register. A week from now—why tomorrow perhaps—he'd be getting kidded about it, and that was all it would amount to. As for the woman . . .

Say—it was a pretty good sort of a rig—this wagon. For the first time in his life—and he hoped devoutly that it would be the last—he was the enforced guest of the police department of a city. He'd ridden with Palsen on the driver's seat of one of the Desplaines' patrols a lot of times, but a single examination of its interior had convinced him that he never wanted a ride inside. It was, as he explained to Dawn, lousy.

And the funny thing about this one was that it wasn't lousy. A fact, he supposed, due to its Evanstonian derivation. Evanston was so blamed high-hat that even its bums were clean. While as for its police department—well—he'd known a lot of cops in his time and he'd met up with a lot of dicks, but he'd be darned if he'd ever struck one as all-fired high-and-mighty as Chief Abeel. To stick handcuffs on a man just because an hysterical woman in a tight place gave the quick lie to his story wasn't white. No Chicago cop'd do it—no New York cop—no . . . by Heaven! no cop who was a cop would do it!

He contemplated that thought for a minute and then glanced at the silent man who sat beside him. His uniform was all right—spick and span enough—and so was the uniform of the man who was driving up in front. Abeel's, too . . . and that was the trouble . . . they were too spick and span to be true. The sort of uniforms that stage cops wore. And then Abeel—who was Abeel? A new man on the job—an import that nobody'd ever seen. The story had run not two days before that Carlton Abeel had been appointed to fill the vacancy left by the resignation of Evanston's former chief. And who knew him? Who'd seen him? Not Hennery certainly—Hennery who never left the Loop, if he could help it. Hennery would know his name, of course, but wouldn't know the man by sight. And they'd counted on that. He was appalled at the magnitude of his suspicions—at the sheer nerve of such a plan as he was imagining they had put across.

He started to reach for a cigarette and was brought up suddenly to a realization that he had bracelets on his wrists. And they—at least—weren't fake.

"Say, bud," he murmured to the man beside him, "can you give me a pill?"

The other grinned, nodded, and passed one over.

"This Abeel," Kym began cautiously, "he's a new man, isn't he? Stepped into—sa-ay, I haven't been doing Evanston, what's the name of the chief who just got the can?"

"Smith," the other answered with the manner of a man who didn't care.

"Naw," Kym drawled, "it's Jones."

"You got the idea, kid," his captor assured him.

"Hm—quite a trip to the jug—huh?"

"Yep—quite a trip."

Kym was relieved. He had a natural and healthy fear of the law because it worked—and because the whole body of society was back of it—and because it was big enough to carry out any plans it made. But—his eye took in again the patrol he was riding in and he decided that it was a custom job just out of the shop—he wasn't afraid, not for long, of a band of crooks that had tried to put over a game so obvious that even Hennery had seen through it.

And Hennery—why Hennery'd have the laugh on him for a year. And fair enough, too—what a boob he'd been! He laughed, and the man beside him, unbuttoning the tight coat of his unaccustomed uniform, laughed, too.

"Pretty slick, eh?"

"Ye-ah," Kym agreed, "pretty slick. What do you get out of it?"

"Oh—a split—not much. I'm not in with the gang, just took on the job as a fill-in. There's only three of 'em."

"Sure," said Kym, "the woman—this person who pulled the Abeel stunt—and—Meisterberg," he ventured.

"No. Meisterberg's on the level. That is, as far as I know. He's paying cash for the stuff and not asking any questions—that's all. It's Watson who's been doing all the dirty work, I guess. At least he gave orders for this bunch of stuff—wagon and all. But, of course, it's her brains that engineered the thing—and she bumped off the doctor all right. I don't know about Bothwell. I guess he was trying to put over a little private stunt of his own. But you can search me who killed him—doesn't look like a woman's job. It took a good arm to throw that."

"The man who's playing Abeel?"

"No—no—he was on the job early this morning for her call. Figured she was getting out with the dope and I don't think he counted on another killing to gum things up. They had to work fast all right." He chuckled.

"Ever think," Kym ventured, "about going straight?"

"Ye-ah—some. I used to be a regular guy—set type for a small town printer. But the linotype put me out of a job and I just drifted into this. It's easy . . . and the pay's good . . ."

"Sometimes."

"Ever get sent up?"

"No. They never got me. Haven't been working at it long. Figure I'll pile up a little more and then I'll hunt me a job. Got a girl, sort of a good kid, makes good dough-nuts."

"Yes," said Kym, "she sure does."

They laughed.

"Say," Kym observed casually, "maybe Elliot could fix you up in the shop. A guy who knows how to set type can make himself pretty handy around the *Leader*. There's a lot of stuff a machine can't do."

"Jeez! Think you could get me a job?"

Kym thrust his manacled wrists under the other's nose.

"Not with these things on," he said.

His companion glanced apprehensively through the driver's window of the fake patrol. He jerked his head.

"I don't know how he stands," he said. "He's an old-timer and maybe he'd croak us both if he thought we was giving 'em the dirt."

"Scared?" asked Kym.

"No!"

So once more Kym thrust his wrists at the other.

Cautiously a key was produced and as cautiously turned in the lock of the handcuffs. Kym didn't move a muscle. The manacles remained on his wrists and he continued to sit looking straight ahead of him.

"Reach in my inside coat pocket," he directed in a low voice, "and you'll find a folder of cards. My name's on 'em—below the *Leader's*. Take one and hang onto it. When we get squared away come up and see me. Elliot'll fix you up all right—or see that the shop foreman does it. Now listen, when we haul up to wherever this guy's taking us you get out ahead of me—quiet—and I'll follow with my hands together. The other fellow'll be looking for trouble when I see that he hasn't taken me to the station. I'll kick—but I won't give him any real battle when he's looking for it. I'll walk ahead between the two of you and the minute I start fighting you beat it—see?"

The other nodded.

It was less than five minutes later as near as Kym could judge that the patrol came to a stop and they alighted in the middle of a dusty, rutted road that ran between the sort of scrawny poplars that are indigenous to the soil of subdivisions. A little to the right of them stood a farmhouse with a straggling assortment of outhouses, which Kym recognized, to his surprise, even while the larger part of his mind was occupied with ways and means of escape, as that which stood on the far side of the North Branch a mile or so below Annie Thompson's place. The building now looked deserted, dilapidated, wholly without legitimate use or decent neighbors. He saw that any freedom he might obtain would have to be gained by means of his wits and his own right arm—aided and abetted by the length of his legs. There was no help, he realized, within calling distance.

True to his plan he did the best he could at faking surprise and indignation at the absence of a proper police station. And it seemed to get across. The uniformed mail who had driven him to his destination seized his arm at his first protest and pushed him roughly up the narrow path between two rows of dying elms.

"That's all right. That's all right. You keep your mouth shut, and you'll be all right."

Kym called him all the names he could think of offhand without the impetus of sincerity to stimulate his imagination and, twisting violently from his grasp, gave the wink to the man who was following. He turned instantly and ran back toward the road with an agility and speed that would have made Kym laugh if he'd had time for it. But astonishment and consternation had, for a moment, unnerved his immediate captor, and it was just that apprehended moment that Kym had planned to make use of.

He shook the loosened cuffs from his wrists with one swift jerk and swung his right arm in a long, upward curve. His fist—thin and bony but hard for all that—landed a glancing blow on the side of the other's jaw. Not a good uppercut, not a knockout—but the best he could do under the circumstances, and sufficiently powerful to bring the other to his knees. Then, with one leap of his long legs, Kym was over and away—down the road as fast as he could travel, while four bullets from a badly-aimed revolver whipped through the trees around him.

22
The Net Tightens

In his flight before the bullets of his recent captor's revolver, Kym stumbled onto a deep hollow in the uneven
ground of the field. It had once, apparently, been a gravel-
pit. But, long since abandoned, the sides were grown deep
and fragrant with wild-flowers and long grass. At the bottom a small pool had formed, augmented by the recent
rains, and surrounding it with the delicate, gray-green of
their stirring branches, a group of young willows found
water to assuage the thirst of their roots.

Kym slid over the edge of the embankment and down
the slippery grass of its side until his feet encountered the
temporary security of the close-grown willow shoots. Here
he remained for several minutes, panting for breath and
listening intently for a repetition of the shots. None came!
There was no sound save the drowsy hum of a natural
world grown nearly still in noontide heat. Then he heard
the staccato beat of a motor, the explosive irritation of a
backfire, and finally the rhythmic mounting of its speed
as the gears were shifted.

He sighed. The fake patrolman had given up and was
getting his punk patrol out of the way as fast as he could.
He could not know, of course, what his fellow conspirator
who had obviously double-crossed him might still have
up his sleeve. He could not know what Kym's intentions

were—or his capabilities. And he was, Kym supposed, more sold on the idea of saving his skin than of recapturing the escaped reporter.

The pit where Kym was hidden was off the main road by several hundred yards, and its location screened by the poplars along the way. He was secure, he knew, and would be wise to stay until the last sound of the engine had died away. Of course, the man would abandon the fake patrol as soon as possible. Meantime, Kym decided to consider his situation and make plans.

If, as he was now firmly convinced was the case, Amelia Bothwell's plan had been only to give herself time and not, actually, either to harm or keep him in captivity for long, he would be safe in appearing again on the streets. He had to assure himself, as a man waking from a nightmare, that the Evanston police were not even slightly interested in putting him in jail. In fact he realized, now that his mind was getting back to normal, that the Evanston police would be more than glad to see him and interested to learn—although with a degree of astonishment and anger which it amused him to imagine—that a group of crooks had been working an impersonation stunt that included the almighty Chief Abeel himself.

Meantime, of course, Hennery would be busy trying to hunt up facts that would clear Kym—and implicate the woman. But Hennery would not have the evidence that Kym had just acquired about the impersonation stunt. Only a peculiar set of circumstances could possibly bring him the facts. While he was busy—probably in Chicago—trying to get Kym out of the scrape, the woman and the crook would be able to get away—if they hadn't done it already. It was up to Kym to stop them.

A clever plan! A clever woman! Kym was sure she had killed her husband and that she knew where the cat was hidden. Probably in the garden where she had said she walked immediately before breakfast. Digging up the rose-beds! Weeding geraniums! Oh, yes! A clever woman!

Kym's knowledge of medicine was extremely limited—a catch-as-catch-can sort of knowledge picked up in the course of a few dozen killings he'd run into as a reporter. That was all. He'd seen the wounds of death a lot of times, but he didn't know much about the time element involved. In a general way he had known, when he looked at the body of the late Alton Bothwell as it lay on the Persian rug in the library, that death had occurred some time before. The rapidly darkening blood had told him that. But how long before? He couldn't guess.

The professor's wife had said she'd eaten breakfast alone, and it struck Kym, now, that she was a woman who would have found it perfectly possible to eat breakfast after having killed her husband and hidden the precious, radium-bearing cat that had been in his possession in a place of safety. Her pruning of the roses, in fact, may well have been a cover for hiding that container of two hundred thousand dollars worth of rare mineral!

She had hoped, doubtless, to get the other cat from Kym. Or at any rate his written release to the safety deposit vault that he had rented—like a dumb fool—for her convenience. Then she'd have the entire fortune! Four hundred thousand dollars worth of radium! And no takers! Well . . .

Kym found his position increasingly uncomfortable. The fake patrol had had plenty of time to clear the neighborhood and he felt he'd better be on his way. With extreme caution, and inch by inch, he worked himself around so that he was lying face down on the steep embankment, his feet still firmly braced against the branches of the willow. Grasping the brief security of successive handfuls of waving grass, he pulled himself up to the edge.

Once more on firm ground, he paused to get his bearings. He was not familiar with this side of the river. The land was the property of a subdivision company and not of Cook county, like the stretch over the way. He had rarely crossed the bridge that led to this portion. He didn't know quite where he was. He looked in the direction where he thought the abandoned farmhouse must be but couldn't locate it. Nevertheless, he started out with his long, loping walk, hoping to find the river.

As he walked, his mind, relieved, for the time of more material considerations, turned to Dawn. He remembered Hennery's remark just before he left to effect Kym's rescue. The remark about Dawn Carson—and how she'd interview the devil himself to save Kym. Coming from Hennery— staid, unemotional, hard-boiled Hennery—it was funny enough. But coming from any source it would equally have knocked Kym off his feet at once if more desperate concerns had not shelved it for the time. Now it was on the table again.

"Dawn Carson'd interview the devil, himself, to save you!"

Lord! It was a fundamental truth. He recognized it. Loyal, fearless Dawn—Dawn, his good friend! Dawn . . .

His feeling for her had grown so gradually, so gently, in a keen delight in her companionship, that he had been taking it for granted. Like his pipe. A habit! She had won his liking and his respect, and so—in accordance with his somewhat unique and rigid code—he hadn't touched her. Except for Dead River. And that—well—the shock of that had unnerved him for almost a week, and then he'd decided to relegate even the thought of it to a later date when he knew more about how he felt concerning this girl among girls.

Hennery's statement had served to crystallize his thoughts and feelings about her. He knew, now, that Dawn fell into a category in which no other girl had ever been placed as far as he was concerned. He loved her! Lord! And when you loved a girl the way he knew, now, he loved Dawn, you married her. And that was that! If . . . if . . . she'd marry you!

But why in Sam Hill should she? His salary wasn't bad, but no girl'd marry him for it—sure! His habits, when it came to alcohol and gambling were not of the sort that made for happy homes. But when he thought about her as he had seen her a hundred times—talked, walked and argued with her, realized that, even now, she was probably working with her brave and cheerful energy to get him out of a scrape, he decided, once and for all, to cut out booze—to cut out craps—to cut out . . . He shook, his head and grinned. No girl—not any girl with Dawn's sane attitude toward life would expect him altogether to give up poker!

He looked up suddenly to find himself on the near side of the bridge that spanned the river. He recognized the country now. He crossed the bridge and started out for the street that led to a car line. He felt in his pockets. At least the bums hadn't cleaned him, and he'd been lucky at cards the day before. If he could find a taxi he'd be all set.

He walked half a mile and ran a block to hail a passing cab. He gave as his directions the headquarters for Evanston police and was there in record-breaking time—at a premium.

Hennery and the chief received him with shouts. The real chief—Carlton Abeel, himself—very hurt as to dignity and very determined as to action concerning the clever crook who had had the unmitigated nerve to attempt an impersonation of the chief of police of Chicago's most snooty suburb.

Hennery, it seems, had smelled a rat because the man who was supposed to be chief of Evanston was wearing such an elaborate uniform.

"We're dumb, boy," he told Kym, "just plain dumb not to have seen through it right off. The big guys don't dress up—and you know it and so do I."

So he'd poked his nose into Evanston headquarters not ten minutes after Kym had been carted off in what was supposed to be an Evanston patrol. And so, of course, the story broke. It only needed Kym's tale of his abduction and escape to clinch the matter and furnish the details.

The chief got two patrolmen in tow and all five of them set off at once for the house of the late Professor Bothwell. In his fastest car Abeel of Evanston drove up silently to a point a block from the house and parked. They climbed out and made their way rapidly and cautiously over the lawn under the quiet and indifferent shadows of the elms.

"We'll just take it easy till we get what he's up to. If we can catch him with the goods so much the better. The bird can't get away from us unless he's flown already, and we'll be the gainers by a little watchful waiting." Chief Abeel pointed to the low Victorian panes at the front of the house. "Those windows, now—what room do they give onto?"

Hennery whispered, "The front parlor where we left this guy and the lady-bird a little while ago. She's in it, too, of course. Smart! That's what—smart!"

"All right!" Abeel cut in sharply. "Down we go on our knees. Approach below the level of the sills—and have your guns ready."

Kym, gunless, joined them on all fours. A press card, he felt, was not the best defense in the world. But still . . . he didn't want to miss anything. Carefully he crawled along the ground until he reached one of the windows. Then, rising slowly, he brought his eyes to a place just above the level of the sill where he could look through the blowing curtains into the green-papered front parlor—

the front parlor that had stiff pink roses on its floor and furniture of walnut and black horsehair.

The late professor's wife was seated on the same chair that she had occupied earlier. Only now a small black hat was on her head and a suitcase stood on the floor beside her. The man whose pretense of being Carlton Abeel had succeeded in deceiving both Hennery and Kym for more than an hour was in front of her, his legs spread wide apart in a manner that suggested solidity of purpose—unwavering determination.

"I haven't got it, Jim! Honestly! I haven't got it!" Amelia Bothwell was repeating in a thin, tired voice that was, somehow, strangely piteous. "I tell you somebody else killed Alton—and got the cat. There's not a penny left! Not a penny! You *must* believe me! You *must!* And help me out of this. Oh! Jim! You're all I've got, now. I've worked with you all the way through . . ."

"Yes," he said grimly, "only to double-cross me in the end. What the devil do you figure I took you on for? Love? Not on your life! I'm in tight enough myself without dragging you around as excess baggage. And if you think you can play me dirty on the loot . . . !"

His face flushed suddenly. His eyes blazed.

"Come out with it! And come damned quick, or by God . . ."

Her hands flew to her face and she cried faintly—in a strained voice, now, of pure terror:

"It's true—oh, it's true! I haven't got . . ."

His revolver, whipped from his pocket, spat out three vicious, deadly bullets. Then it dropped from his hand. A fusillade of shots from outside had echoed his own, and he spun around, clutching his right arm from which the blood ran in a warm, steady stream.

Amelia Bothwell, betrayer and betrayed, was dead when the five men entered the room. But her murderer, his uninjured hand raised high in the air, was face to face with Abeel of Evanston—and with the gleaming muzzle of his revolver.

"Jim Harley! So here's where you headed after the Detroit Savings Bank deal—eh? Well—maybe Mr. Hennery'll recognize you when he sees you out of uniform—and in stripes. Look more like your picture on the records that way—don't you?" He turned, to his patrolmen.

"Give this man the cuffs," he ordered, "and I'll go with him to the station. It'll give me a big kick to watch him booked. And I'm here to tell you that one of the charges'll be that of impersonating an officer."

23

Dawn Carson

She had gone to sleep thinking about Kym, and she had waked up dreaming about him. And when she found her thoughts, during the short, ugly walk to the "L" concentrated on him again, she gave herself up in disgust. Accustomed to facing life as a series of fairly hard facts that could be softened only slightly by a modicum of charm, she seldom lied to Dawn Carson.

When, in the earlier days of her self-support, she had received fifteen dollars a week as a file clerk, she had forced herself to the habit of regarding a hat, for instance, strictly as a hat, and rent, on the other hand, as rent. So that, when deciding to buy a hat instead of paying the rent she had never done so under the delusion that her landlady would suddenly develop a golden vein of charity in the dark ore of her nature. If she bought the hat she went straight to the landlady and told her about it—and told her, too, that two weeks' rent would be forthcoming on the next due-day. Which, as this same landlady always discovered, it invariably was. All of which, she was ready to admit, was a compromise with fate but not a dishonest compromise.

She had, in the course of the last three years, pulled herself out of the fifteen-dollar-a-week class by some forty-five additional dollars, but she had never lost the habit, cultivated in the lean months, of telling the truth to the landlady.

The landlady in this case, she discovered as she found herself examining a basket of spinach and wondering why it had to be twenty cents a pound again in August, was Dawn Carson. And she knew that, right now, she would have to tell Dawn Carson what she knew. She knew she was in love with Kym—foolishly, romantically, idealistically in love. She was so much in love that she would be glad to quit digging up good features for the *Leader,* glad to leave behind her all the exciting, nerve-pricking life of the office and the Loop if thereby she might be privileged to cook spinach (at twenty cents a pound) for Kym—who doubtless wouldn't eat it. She knew that she would accept the fact that he drank too much occasionally, as well as the knowledge that he shot craps and sometimes lost half a week's wages at a night of poker, if only she could have him—sure enough—for long hikes up the Lake shore on all the Sundays of her life, for evenings before open fires in the wide wood-spaces of the North Branch—for mornings when he'd be cussing to himself as he shaved his blond young skin, and cut it, or singing as he bathed. She knew she would be willing—if she listened only to the foolish, senseless pounding of her heart when he was near—to bring six successive babies into a world where a ninety-dollar contract was the highest rung of the immediate ladder. And she knew that she was a fool.

For if she married Kym—and he'd shown no definite sign that he had any intention of wanting to marry her— she would have to keep on working or lose her mind. If she married Kym, she would want to keep on living as comfortably as she was living now, in a small apartment or, at best, in a tiny house in the suburbs. And her only chance of keeping him the way he was—with all his yellow-haired innocent sophistication—would be to go to work with him each morning and come home with him at night.

She paused to stamp her foot on the elevated platform where she waited for her morning train. She'd be darned if she was going to trust herself with any man who would make such a fool of himself as John Kymmerly had done over the professor's clever wife. He'd got himself in wrong for sure this time—unless he could manage to get hold of the other cat—the cat he had so nonchalantly ("and there's your innocent sophistication") handed over to the professor the day before. Two hundred thousand dollars! Why the idiot needed a guardian—he needed her. She would never have taken the cock-and-bull story of a woman in a red dress for the truth—and let herself become involved at that. Yes, Kym certainly needed her to keep him out of mischief.

She giggled as she thought of proposing to him on just that basis—and caught the smiling eyes of a platform guard as she stepped onto her express.

"Nice day," she remarked.

"Ye-ah, ye-ah, getting a bit fallish, though."

He closed the door with a bang and came to sit beside her. On the way to the office she had no more chance to think of Kym, for her ears were regaled for half an hour with a detailed account of just why the first dropping of the maple leaves on September fourth should indicate a heavy fall of snow at Christmas. But by way of revenge she got his name and wrote a snappy story a day or so later on "A Prophet Without Honor."

It was nine o'clock when she landed in the City Room, a good hour, all considered, for Dawn Carson to appear.

"Kym been in?" she asked.

"Yep," said Elliot without looking up, "and out again."

She walked slowly across the floor.

"Say, Miss Carson," it was Leffingwell's voice calling
from the little cubby-hole where he pasted his column together every day, "can you come here a minute?"

Dawn stood in his doorway.

Leffingwell looked at her with a paternal air not quite
warranted by his five gray hairs, and shook his head. "Got
a bad case, haven't you, kid? Well—so's he—so's he—only
he doesn't know it yet. Now when I was young . . ."

"Have you got anything to say to me, or haven't you? If
you haven't, I'm going to get a start on a story."

"Oh! Yes—now . . . let's see . . . what was I going . . .
say, listen," he suddenly removed his hands from behind
his head, and let his chair drop forward on its front legs,
"I was going to tell you that I think your boy friend's in
bad. Elliot wouldn't let us in on the whole story, but between Kym's expression and the chief's wild call—together
with what we managed to overhear—I gather that the lad
is in for a grand larceny charge if he doesn't move fast. I
don't know just what . . ."

But she was gone—had left the door of the cubicle in a
single, sweeping turn and was half way across the room in
the direction of the city editor's desk before Leffingwell
had finished his sentence.

"I thought that'd fetch her," he remarked so that she
faintly heard him. "I'd like to see 'em get it over with.
Always makes me nervous to watch 'em making up their
minds. Now if anybody'd bag Kymmerly for grand larceny
. . . !" He laughed and returned to pasting somebody else's
jokes in the next day's column.

She stood directly in front of Elliot's desk and demanded his attention. Elliot liked her—thought her a good writ-
er and more nearly level-headed than most of the women
he'd had on the staff—but all women were alike when it
came to business and, if it weren't for the sob stuff he

wouldn't have 'em around. Always mixing business with pleasure, confusing emotion and morals.

"Well?" he grumbled.

"What's the story about Kym?"

He leaned back in his chair and thrust his hands in his pockets. There was a pencil behind his ear and an ink-smudge on his nose.

"Now who's been stirring you all up? Leffingwell? Leffingwell can mind his own business. The bunch of you will have me bugs around here pretty soon. First that young fool—and so damned good a reporter that I can't fire him without giving him a chance to save his own skin—gets himself all wound up in a mess with a pair of green cats, a lot of radium and a couple of murders and then . . ."

"A couple of murders!"

"Oh God! I knew I'd let myself in . . . Now if you'll keep your young mouth shut, I'll let you in on the yarn. Sit down, Miss Carson," he added in a kinder tone as he saw the genuine concern in her face.

He spent some minutes in telling her the story, preceding it by assuring her that he didn't have the time, and he didn't fail to remember that she had had some part in it, particularly in the discovery concerning the contents of the cats. When he finished, he said:

"Run along and get me out two columns on the Working Girls' Camp. And don't forget that Kincaid is backing it." He took his pencil from behind his ear and then called after her, "I'll let you know if anything comes up about the boyfriend. Now forget it."

She couldn't forget it, but she concentrated her efforts sufficiently so that when, at a few minutes before twelve, Elliot answered the phone on his desk and shortly afterwards summoned her, she had completed a couple of thousand words of eulogy about a subject of which she knew absolutely nothing.

It was Hennery who wanted her—a Hennery strangely agitated.

"Miss Carson?"

"Yes."

"This is Mr. Hennery—Ogden Hennery of the Bureau. I'm out in Evanston—just left the Bothwell place—and there's some dirty work being pulled. They've got your friend, Kymmerly—carted him away, and I'm going straight from here to Evanston headquarters to find out about it."

She gave a small gasp and then said, faintly, "Yes, Mr. Hennery."

"Want to help him get out, don't you?"

"Oh—yes!" Her voice was no longer faint.

"Well—here's, what I want you to do. You can't help about getting him out of the hoosegow—but you may be able to get some dope on the Bothwell woman that'll put her in. And if she gets in, he'll get out.

"Go to Annie Thompson's place—she's soft on Kymmerly anyway—and tell her the whole yarn. If she comes clean with everything she knows—and I'll warrant she knows a lot she isn't telling—I think it'll fix things for us. I'll meet you there as soon as I can get away. Good luck."

The receiver clicked at the other end of the line. He was gone, and she'd had no opportunity to ask questions—to discover anything as to Kym's welfare, the conditions under which he had been taken to Evanston headquarters. Headquarters! Kym arrested and confined by force in a police station! The idea would have been ludicrous if it had not been appalling. Yet she knew from experience that he had both physical agility and mental skill in getting himself out of tight places. He was guilty of nothing—of that she was certain; Hennery was back of him now and she—she was for him a hundred per cent ("until Hell freezes") she told herself. And with that acknowledgment she accepted the implications of her fate.

She picked up her hat, slipped into the brief jacket of her black moire suit (a suit that Kym could not have bought any week after he'd paid the rent) and went directly to Elliot's desk.

"Yes," he said, "I got it. Hennery told me the dope before he talked to you. Go ahead—and get that bum out of trouble if you can. Oh—by the way—where's the Camp story? It's got to run this afternoon."

She handed it to him and walked rapidly through the dark, low-ceilinged room to the rickety door that led onto a flight of dilapidated stairs. Running down, she called a greeting to the elevator man as he passed her, and flew past the cashier's window with a nod.

Once out on the sidewalk she searched the cobble-paved street for a taxi. For the first time in her life as a reporter she failed to see half a dozen at least scurrying around the corner or flashing by on the cross-street. Each moment was an agonizing hour, and she had no intention of prolonging the misery by submitting to the slow progress of the "L" and a couple of street cars. She wanted a taxi, she wanted it desperately; and none came.

At last her searching eyes made out the color of a cab a block away on the other side of the street standing in front of what she knew to be a restaurant. She ran the full distance, crossed the street between two speeding trucks and burst into the lunch room.

"If you'll eat your sandwich on the way and get me where I want to go—quick—I'll give you a dollar over the fare," she cried.

The man at the counter swallowed his coffee in one gulp, flung a dime and two nickels on the counter and dashed out ahead of her.

"Where to?" he mumbled through a mouthful of thick, white bread interpenetrated with minced ham.

And it was not until then that she discovered that she didn't know "where to." She knew where Annie Thompson's place was, of course, had a very clear and loving picture of it in her mind, but she hadn't the faintest idea of what street ran past its picket fence, of what car-line led nearest its entrance. She had visited it only once and then with Kym by way—it was true—of the familiar river along whose banks she had walked often and for many miles. But of how to approach it in the more ordinary way of city dwellers she hadn't the least notion. There was in the face of this predicament only one thing to do—to direct the driver to the red-brick schoolhouse at which she and Kym most frequently got off the car, and down the street that crossed the car line until its end was reached. Here, where the pavement of the city gave way to the gently rolling country of the forest preserve, she would have to leave him and make the rest of the way on foot.

"Out Lawrence," she directed him, "to Kostner, and when we come to Kostner I'll tell you the rest of the way."

He reached Broadway by a series of irrational, northwest jogs and dodged street cars for miles. When, finally he turned west onto the comparative quiet of Lawrence Avenue, Dawn breathed a sigh of relief. She was nearly there now, nearly at any rate, at the point where her walk would have to begin, and her watch told her it was only half past twelve.

Ten minutes later he let her out, not without a look of wonder in his eyes, at the end of the paved street that gave directly on a muddy road. She paid him the three-twenty he asked for without bothering to look at the meter and thrust an extra dollar into his hand as she started to run.

Down the first gentle swell of grass that had turned to a sudden, fresh green under the last few days of unexpected rain, along the narrow, winding path that led beside the river, over the first bridge, and through an interminable

half mile of cut-over woodland and small brush, through
a cornfield and over the second bridge.

At last through the trailing willows and stray elms that
shaded the bank of the sluggish stream, she caught sight
of a farmhouse on the other shore. It was familiar to her,
precious and dear, for all its disorderly array of straggling
outbuildings and unkempt yard, because in sight of it Kym
and she had often camped. And she remembered, now, that
Annie Thompson's house was not much more than a mile
away. Her feet that had been lagging with weariness took
new hope at this, and she began to run again.

Then suddenly she stopped dead still, her hand at her
throat and her quick, brown eyes opened wide in terror.
Four shots had been fired very near her—they had seemed,
in fact, to come from the direction of the farmhouse. Four
shots in rapid succession and followed by a shout that
was either rage or pain. She remained unmoving for a full
two minutes, but there was no other sound. Then, just as
she began cautiously to move forward again there followed
the noise of an automobile starter spinning, the hiccup of
its engine as it caught and began to run, and finally the
enraged futility of a loud backfire.

Not strange sounds, certainly, to be heard in an ordinary city street, but very strange sounds indeed in this
section of wood and deserted farmland that had been re-
served as a playground for city dwellers. There were few
roads here and those few obscure and badly rutted. There
had been no one, she had noticed on a previous visit with
Kym, about the grounds or near the desolate house.

Slowly, then, as a last staccato emphasis of the engine
died away, she began to walk again—a little less secure—a
little more convinced that life can be both serious and
horrible. She passed the farmhouse and had mounted the
steep embankment of the third bridge when, on the other
side and across the river from where she stood, she saw

a man lying on the ground at the water's edge. She drew back—made uncustomarily timid by the late sound of gunfire and slowly it came home to her that the quiet figure was very quiet indeed. It had not moved, and was lying too awkwardly for comfort, one hand trailing helplessly in the muddy water of the stream.

She crept forward slowly, then, driven by wonder and held back by fear. She recalled the shots that she had heard, and the memory filled her with an ever greater terror. She changed her course and used the bridge to cross over, sliding and tumbling in a sudden access of dreadful haste, her mind recently so filled with thoughts of him that her fevered imagination had seized on the notion that it might be Kym.

But the body on the ground by the water's edge was not his. It was that of a boy who must have been about fourteen, emaciated and in rags. That he was dead was evident to her at once, but what filled her with even greater shrinking was the realization that he had died very recently—within the last few minutes probably. The blood was still flowing—very bright red—from between his lips. She could not see where he had been struck. He was lying half turned over on his side as though he had struggled once before he died, and one hand was clutched tightly against his body.

Dawn gave a little cry and bent over quickly, forgetful of the blood, forgetful that violent death had lately visited this scene. For in the boy's hand, was securely clasped the figure of a jade-green cat.

24

Hot Copy

It was not altogether surprising, considering the time element involved, that the three people on the outside who were most deeply interested in the Cartwright case should have arrived at Annie Thompson's almost simultaneously.

Abeel of Evanston had taken Jim Harley in tow, pausing only long enough to explain to Hennery and Kym that this was the man wanted in several cities for various recent high-grade thefts.

"They've got a report on him at headquarters," Hennery agreed. "I've heard the name, but I don't go over the gallery very often and I didn't know him by sight. Besides, he's never operated in Chicago before."

"No—he's been working Detroit—getting more than his share of gold-brick stuff, and he's pulled some other stunts almost as elaborate as this. That fellow's talent is wasted off the stage."

"A picker-up, eh?" Hennery asked. "The guy that flirts with women on the mezzanine of a Loop hotel—and gets their stories. You know I wouldn't be surprised if that female's yarn was true up to the point where she failed to tell us about running onto this bozo. She might have been full of moral indignation and all that—gradually undermined by the idea of so much of the goods handy. Remember what she said, Kymmerly, about how a realization of the value of radium would go to your head? She was talking about her husband, but it applies just as well to herself. I suppose if she hadn't been convinced there was a ready market for it, she'd never have stepped in.

"And as for the old guy's death—the doctor's—I don't know—that may very well have been accidental in a sense. A man in as bad condition as he was would be likely to go with very little help. Bothwell's threat, or the disappearance of half the small fortune from his bag—either one might have been enough to finish him—although an overdose of thyroid would finish the thing. I wonder . . .

"Your men didn't find the other cat, did they?" he asked Abeel just before the other started toward his car. And when a negative answer was returned he nodded. "I thought not. In fact, I'd have been pretty much surprised if they had. That woman didn't kill her husband, and when she died she was telling the truth—for once.

"There come your men, and that releases all of us to go about our business. I suppose you'll take care of the two bodies, eh? Hardly my territory."

He smiled, and lifted his hat. "Come on, Kymmerly," he said, and they walked to the small, powerful roadster that waited a block away.

"The girl friend's probably out at Annie Thompson's now," he continued as they drove south. "I shipped her there to find what she could get on the Bothwell woman. I thought they had you in the coop, sure."

"Lord!" said Kym, "so did I for a few minutes. And nothing ever gave me the creeps more. When I discovered it was just a bunch of gun-shooting crooks I picked up hope. You know, Hennery, I've been a most considerable damned fool and I hope it's taught me to stop trusting women."

"Oh, I don't know, I don't know," said Hennery ruminatively. "This Carson girl, now . . ."

"Dawn Carson! Dawn's different."

"Ye-ah, that's how I thought you felt about her," said Hennery as he swung the car around a corner and headed east off Green Bay road.

They were both quiet for several minutes as though the allusion to Kym's feelings for a girl had embarrassed them both. It was Kym who first broke the silence.

"Who do you think's got the other cat?" he asked. "And do you figure we'll get it back? You know I've had both of 'em in my hands not long since and I'm kind of leery about being held responsible. It's going to take a lot of talking to convince the Radium Society that I didn't know there was a fortune in 'em."

"No, it isn't," said Hennery. "No, it isn't. Your looks are in your favor. Nobody who looks as simple as you do . . ." They both laughed and the tension was broken. "Besides which," Hennery continued, "I've got a notion that stuff's going to turn up pretty soon. I wouldn't like to swear who's got it now, but I'll bet it won't take long to find it."

"Meisterberg?" Kym asked.

"No—boy—no. And now I'll tell you something. I don't know just who this guy, Meisterberg, is, but I do know he's not just what he pretends to be. Headquarters told me hands off him as much as six months ago, and when I found he was mixed up in the Cartwright killing I went straight to Leeming. Leeming and I usually work together pretty well and he doesn't keep me in the dark unless there's a reason.

"'That's all right,' Leeming told me. 'He'll work better if he's let alone, and it'll only ball things up if you give him any publicity. And if you bump into him on the street, pretend you don't know him.'

"Sa-ay, you thought you had something on me when you found he was staying at the Congress, didn't you? I had to threaten to fire three of my men before they'd learn to quit reporting him on Michigan Avenue."

Kym looked his astonishment. "But why have you kept on hounding Annie Thompson? The old girl's innocent or I'm a dumb-bell."

"You're a dumb-bell all right," Hennery agreed, "but I've got to agree with you I think she's not mixed up in it personally. But did you ever stop to think about mother love and all that stuff? Sounds like the bunk till you run against it. Take a woman who's so honest she wouldn't touch a penny that didn't belong to her—and then see what she'll do when she has a son. She'll lie, steal and commit murder to keep him out of trouble."

"But the boy's loony," Kym objected.

"Ye-ah, loony enough, and all the more reason why she'd let herself be burned at the stake, if it would save him. Mother love—it's a funny thing. She might not steal for him, but she might feel perfectly justified in lying about it, if he did. And so would you, Kymmerly, in the same circumstances—so would we all."

"But why should he go after the radium—if that's what you think he did. He hasn't sense enough to know what to do with it."

"I don't know. That's one of the things I haven't been able to figure out. But I'm basing that, too, on a fundamental motive, because fundamental motives are the foundation of all crimes: love of the sort that's an obsession, hate that's often the outcome of such love, greed, and self-preservation. You can analyze 'em all you please in any elaborate way that suits your fancy, but they'll simmer down to those four in the end.

"Suppose this boy Sandy loved his mother about the way a dog loves his master—without much reasoning about it or much figuring on why or how—but just blind- ly devoted as a half-wit boy would be. Then suppose he got the notion that his mother was being cheated—treated dirty. Mind, I'm not saying that's what happened; but, if it was, wouldn't he do anything to square things for her? He might not think it out—might simply follow through on what he figured would give her what she wanted. See?"

Yes, Kym saw, in part. But he couldn't reduce the general to the particular in this case. He couldn't see how the jade-green cats could have been made to hook up in Sandy's mind with the idea of justice to his mother. And even if he could—what good would it do? Sandy was the one person still wholly missing from the solution of the Cartwright case, and likely to remain missing as far as any evidence to the contrary was concerned.

But wasn't there evidence to the contrary? The second of the cats that he had found in Annie Thompson's garden (was it only night before last?) might very logically have been put there by the boy. And if that were true he must be some place in the neighborhood. Suddenly Kym slapped his leg.

"By George!" he said, "I'll bet you're right." And then he told of the small incident, until now buried in the lower strata of his mind by all the startling events of the last couple of days, when he had returned to the camp-fire beside which he had eaten his meal with Dawn two nights before.

"I went back after my pipe that I'd left on the ground and just as I came into the ring of light a youngster that I should judge to have been about fourteen, jumped back after having grabbed a hunk of bread we'd thrown away. We weren't a mile from Annie Thompson's then, and it was this same night that I found the cat in her garden. Two bits the boy was Sandy. Lord! He looked starved."

Hennery nodded.

"And by the way," the notion suddenly occurred to Kym, "did you ever clear up the mystery of the missing elevator?"

Hennery laughed out loud. "Sure," he said, "and that was a joke on Watson. You see these foreign women who cleaned up the offices were all scared of the cheap crook. They had used the elevator at night for a long time, but they didn't want him to know it. They'd get their pails and soap and stuff in the basement and run themselves up to the tenth floor. Then they'd work down—and the last ones off the tenth floor always brought the cage down with 'em. Well, that night—or morning—they got so all-fired flustered they forgot to bring the thing down before they called the police. And when Watson got there they were too scared to tell us about it—Watson, the almighty janitor being present."

"Then I suppose the footprints on the roof didn't hook up with the elevator as we figured they did at first," Kym contributed eagerly. "The guy that made 'em must have climbed up the fire-escape and robbed Cartwright of one of the cats—then gone on up to the roof and so down through the trap-door and out the building. Is that it?"

"That's just about it as near as we can figure out—and as near as we'll ever know, I guess, unless we can get Sandy cornered."

But they were destined, of course, never to get Sandy cornered—not a live Sandy who could, however inadequately, answer their questions. Just as Hennery brought the car to a stop in front of Annie Thompson's white picket gate, a breathless and terrified Dawn came tearing through the back garden, around the potting shed, over the cold-frames—crying and stumbling as she ran. In her hand on which, to her ever-mounting horror, were great streaks of drying blood, she held the second of the jade-green cats.

Hennery took the whole thing calmly enough, merely remarking that now there'd be another corpse to look after because this was in his territory; but Kym was overcome with a great relief, a sense of infinite well-being, an overwhelming tenderness.

The one thing he really dreaded was the necessity of breaking the news to Annie, but Annie must, by this time, be so accustomed to the idea of Sandy's loss that so small a certainty as the possession of his body to be buried in consecrated ground would be a source of some contentment to her.

And he had a plan in the back of his head that he wanted to put up to Dawn as soon as he could be alone with her for long—preferably out of doors—a plan that included Annie Thompson and Annie Thompson's little house and her geraniums and her delphiniums and Dawn's beloved hollyhocks. He looked at these latter now as they approached the front door of Annie's cottage and decided that they were, after all, not bad.

But the ultimate surprise awaited Kym in Annie's front parlor. Only Hennery did not seem to be put out by the presence of Karl Meisterberg in that place so far from the scene of his supposed activities.

"Meisterberg?" he asked. "We haven't met, but we ought to know each other. I'm Hennery of the Bureau. Leeming told me when I phoned him a while ago that you'd be out here when we arrived."

He introduced the others, and Karl Meisterberg bowed as he greeted them.

"Miss Carson," he said, and Kym realized that it was the first time he'd ever heard the voice of the man about whom there had been so much controversy, "perhaps you will be good enough to relieve yourself of the burden of the cat when you hear what I have to tell you. I wish to assure you that the sight of it is very pleasant to my eyes."

Annie, of course, had to be told as gently as possible by a Dawn who was, herself, frankly crying—about Sandy's death. Kym assured her that he must have died almost at once—and so he had not suffered. And he told her, further, that the bullet that hit the boy must have been meant for himself.

"We must just have missed each other in the wooded strip near the farmhouse," Kym told her, "because the fellow who had taken me fired four times—and always just a little too far to the right."

"Since it had to be Sandy," she said with a degree of fatalism, "I'm glad it missed hitting you, Mr. Kym—for I've grown fond of the two of you while this awful time's been going on.

"But where would Sandy get the cat?" she wanted to know with such obvious honesty of ignorance that Hennery's theory about her complicity was hit promptly on the head.

"I think I can answer that question for you," Karl Meisterberg put in, "almost as well as Mr. Hennery—and as it's getting well past noon and I'll warrant none of you has eaten much since morning—I'd better get my story told and be on my way."

Annie's eyes were drying rapidly and she said, somewhat mournfully:

"When you've brought the boy to me, I'll fix you all up a snack in the kitchen. A body's got to eat, come death or not . . ."

Hennery telephoned headquarters and assured her that two men with an ambulance would be out from the nearest station in a few minutes. "But perhaps you would rather go and wait beside him until they come," he said kindly. "This man's story can be retold to you if there's any need."

"My narrative will be short enough," Karl Meisterberg began when she had left them, and his enunciation was the careful speech of a man to whom English is a foreign tongue, "because I know that you have most of the facts already in hand. It only remains for me to fill in the holes. Is not that the way you would say it?

"I am an Austrian by birth, but I early became attached to the government of Rungaria. Perhaps it is that I have a taste for diplomacy—intrigue; but at any rate I could find more interest in the court of a small kingdom than in the universities of a big one. Or possibly it is that I prefer to be the big frog in the little pond.

"At any rate I came over here on the mission for my king that I know you have already heard about. But my idea was not to obtain the radium secretly. That is Cartwright's little embroidery to save his face. I went directly to the Radium Society and arranged for a loan of a sufficient quantity to serve my purpose. While I was there the man to whom I talked, one of the officials, told me that a series of radium thefts had been committed recently and that they were very anxious to find the thief because from the nature of the series, their regularity and continuity, it was strongly suspected that a definite plot was on foot, that some single individual was stealing small quantities from various doctors in different parts of the country in order to amass a large amount to be converted into money.

"The fact did not impress me particularly at the time, as I had to communicate at once with the man who had accompanied me on my voyage so as to acquaint him with the successful completion of my arrangements. He returned to our hotel and I went to make a call on Amos Cartwright whom I had not seen since my university days.

"I told him of my mission, but had not yet informed him of my agreement with the Radium Society when he declared excitedly that he could save me money on such a transaction. He offered me some four hundred thousand dollars worth of radium (for it was more than five grams that I had planned to take back with me) for three hundred thousand dollars.

"'And you can sell it at a profit when it has done its work,' he offered as an inducement.

"This suggestion recalled to me the story I had heard of the thefts that had taken place. I asked Amos where he could obtain such an amount and at such a price—for the standard of value has been set by the Radium Society—but he only assured me that his knowledge of its source would be to my profit and that I had better be content with that. Also he stipulated that I wait six months more for my supply.

"Now the progress of cancer in its early stages is not swift, but when it has reached the point to which my king's illness had arrived, its inroads are rapid and terrible. So I could not have waited in any case. But, after considering the matter for a while, I told him that I would let him know of my decision on the following day. His answer was a self-conscious smile and some reference to 'honor among friends.'

"At the time of our greatest intimacy Amos had been little more than an acquaintance and I felt that now, if he had so degenerated as to stoop to the role of thief, my loyalty was toward society rather than toward him. Radium is a great agency for good, a great instrument in the hands of scrupulous men, but diverted from its various channels by a man whose whole impulse is that of greed, it can grow to evil.

"I returned at once to the office of the Radium Society and told them what I had learned, and that I had every reason to believe that Amos Cartwright was the man they sought. And they asked me to undertake the task of cornering him.

"I agreed, but first I saw the companion of my travels and hastened him on his way to take the blessed mineral to our king. Then, with my message concerning my temporary occupation in this country safely directed to those people to whom I owed my first allegiance, I set about the business of seeing that justice was rendered the cause of science."

"And your king?" Kym interrupted with an anxiety that could be explained only by the eloquence of this man's genuine sincerity of feeling.

"He is resting, thank you," the other returned with a warmth in his voice, "better."

He resumed his tale: "But now came the difficult part. In order to prove that the vast amount of the mineral that he was going to sell me secretly had been stolen, I had to let him continue to steal it. For even when I had absolute proof from the testimony of such doctors as had been put on their guard against him, I could make no move until I knew where and how he was concealing the stuff. Besides," he shrugged, "what good would his imprisonment have done us if we had failed to find the radium. It was necessary, as I believe you phrase it, to 'get the goods on him?' And it took me the full six months to do it.

"For while I pretended to have returned, temporarily, to my own country I actually remained in this—watching—waiting. And during my one 'return' some three months after our agreement had been made, I learned a good deal. I learned what Amos Cartwright was doing with the boy and I learned, also, that he had worked so on the child's sympathies and credulity as to make him believe that the stuff he was storing in geranium pots and bringing to the doctor on his visits was to be in the nature of a surprise for his mother, a gift of some remarkable sort that was too wonderful for him to understand.

"But the doctor had counted without the fixity of purpose that serves the average subnormal as well in attaining his objective as the so-called 'will' serves normal people. I knew that the boy was bringing in the pots of flowers regularly and the doctor in his eagerness was often careless in removing the small lead safes from the soil in which he had buried them, so that I had plenty of opportunity to observe him. I could not, however, discover where he was storing it. I knew enough about the nature of radium to be sure that they must be kept in some fairly orderly fashion so that the rays would not be lost. But it was not until the night of the séance—the night that, in my last desperate effort to locate the $400,000 worth that had been, by this time, reported stolen, I had fabricated a trip to my own country—that I woke up to the significance of the jade-green cats.

"Sandy must have been sitting in the outer room during my entire conversation with Amos Cartwright on that afternoon. And he had just enough sense to realize that the doctor's proposed trip with me meant that some plan was being carried through to take the precious stuff he had been helping to accumulate for his mother out of the city, out of the country, out of his life . . .

"He had disappeared, as you know, when his mother returned to get him and I am certain that he remained hidden in the alley back of the Umpire Building until dark; until, in fact, our séance gave him the opportunity to enter the inner office by way of the fire-escape. It was only a few minutes before Alton Bothwell and his wife appeared that I saw Cartwright put the two cats carefully in his bag. And it dawned on me that those cats were of lead—and therefore perfect containers (if properly fitted up inside) for a quantity of radium.

"I held my peace, however, until after the guests had gone and then Cartwright told me that the invasion of his inner room during our meeting had been robbery, and that nearly half the mineral had disappeared. I could see no object, now, in concealing from the doctor any longer my true identity, and so I told him. I suppose the man was on the verge of dissolution, nervously, physically and mentally as well as morally, for with this revelation he went all to pieces.

"He accused me of having ruined him; he threatened to kill me; and then in his restless and frantic pacing of the room he came upon the bottle of thyroid tablets. His laugh as he discovered them was diabolic.

"'All right,' he shouted, 'Alton has tried to destroy me and you have succeeded. One of you at least will be forced to pay the penalty for my life.' And with that, and the wildest, most insane expression on his face that I have ever seen, he tipped the contents of the bottle—perhaps five tablets of what I should judge to have been about three grains each onto his tongue and swallowed them at once, draining the last of the cordial that had been left on the table in order to get them down.

"The most outrageous performance I ever expect to see! And one only possible to a man already out of his mind. For the result of that dose of glandular secretion—and one that he surely knew would follow—to a man already cursed with an oversupply in his own body, was a death as horrible as you can imagine. I watched him during the next hour while he talked to me of Sandy, of Annie Thompson, of Watson and of Amelia Bothwell, unburdening his heart of all its sordid store of knowledge and suspicion. Then, when the stuff began to get to his heart he developed all the symptoms of suffocation. I fled before he died—fled in pure terror that you would have thought possible only to a boy who has never yet seen death. Yet I could not stop him—would not stop him if I could. For surely—the last right a man in his desperate situation has in this world is that of leaving it if he so wills."

He shuddered.

"I went the next morning directly to the Society and told them the whole tale, confessed my weakness and carelessness in having let one of the cats slip through my fingers as a result of my childish horror of the doctor's death.

I have seen death before, Mr. Hennery, and it was obviously my duty to have obtained that other precious cat—the
one that was still left in his bag—before I left. Yet such
was the manner of his taking-off that all memory of why I
was there seemed to have left me. You see I did not know,
at first, what he had swallowed—actually thought in fact
that he had, perhaps, been indulging in a dramatic dis-
play—until the symptoms of suffocation filled me with
the terror of realization—and acceptance of the fact.

"When I returned the next day, of course, both the bag
and the cat were gone as well as the doctor's body—and
I read in the papers of the startling death in the Umpire Building. If it had not been for my previous arrangement with the Radium Society and their understanding of
secrecy and cooperation on the part of Chicago's Chief of
Police, I should have been afraid of being implicated. As it
was I pledged them my word that I would get the radium
at any cost. I knew now, at least, where and how it was
kept.

"I traced that cat to the reporter at Desplaines Street
who, by the way, knew nothing of its value I am sure, but
no sooner had I discovered that much than it disappeared.
The cat eluded me as fast as I could trail it. That Mr.
Kymmerly had put it in a safety deposit box Amelia Bothwell told me the day you met us in the lobby of the Sherman. She believed that, with this information, she was
reopening a market for the mineral and promised me her
hearty cooperation in obtaining the other cat. I do not
know how the idea of her affiliation with the Radium
Society entered her head—doubtless a coincidence inspired
by the desperate need of exonerating herself from a net of
murder that seemed, gradually, to be closing around her.

"But I wanted the other cat and I could obtain no
information concerning Sandy from his mother. For a
while I suspected her of hiding him—possibly of helping

him in his concealment of the cat. You see I had every reason to believe that Sandy had stolen it. He was the only
person who knew anything of the radium who had not
been in the outer room that night. I thought of Watson,
of course, but I knew that he was, at worst, only a go-between among some crooks and would be wholly ignorant
of the business of handling such loot as radium. Then,
too, the disposition of the flower-pots, the fact that they
had obviously been searched, made me feel that it was the
boy who knew of their contents who must have been looking for treasure in them.

"And when Annie reluctantly admitted that he had
been forever slyly talking about some fabulous present he
was getting ready for her I knew that I was on the right
trail. To her, of course, it was only another of his childish
fancies.

"But after the young man here," he indicated Kym,
"had sent her to me with his notion of getting information, I knew that the second of the cats had been found by
John Kymmerly in her own back yard the night before. But
I could not get in touch with John Kymmerly. Wherever I
searched for him he eluded me—like the cats—and, finally, following his theoretical route to Professor Bothwell's
house this morning I came upon Sandy who had tracked
him, it seems, like a dog—tracked him better than I had,
at any rate, for he knew what I did not know—that the
second of the cats had already been turned over to the professor by Kymmerly.

"He must, during all this time, have been hiding like
an animal—without food and in fear of his life. There
were too many strange and frightening people forever at
his mother's house even after the mysterious agony of her
disappearance for the several days that she was held by
Hennery, I suppose, for him to feel confident about returning. So he went without food, found shelter where

he could and eventually must have slept in the professor's garden all last night waiting for the daylight that would insure his gaining possession once again of that precious gift for his mother.

"We must not judge the boy too harshly. It is just as well, undoubtedly, that he was killed. Because an investigation would have put him, obviously, in an institution for the criminally insane. And it is much better for Annie that conditions are as they have turned out to be. When he hurled the brick through the professor's window—I didn't see him, but I know, of course, that it was he—his mind, I am certain, was blank of everything save the overpowering necessity of getting the cat. And Annie—poor Annie— what would she have done with it if he had ever brought it to her?

"His death was an accident, but, I should say, a fortunate one, as his life was a tragic mistake. It is through him, perhaps, that this whole chain of circumstances developed, for without him I do not believe that Amos Cartwright would have tried to execute a theft of such magnitude. By never returning directly to his own place of business or living, he felt, I think, that he could escape discovery since no one who might follow him would find a trace of radium on his person or in his luggage after he had had time to visit Sandy and Sandy's red geraniums. The flower pots and the cats were, of course, ideal containers for the small lead safes. Then—still following the line of my supposition—if Amos Cartwright had never started the series of thefts, it is probable that Alton Bothwell would not have been tempted to avarice or his wife dragged into the net of a man whose whole life has been dedicated to the pursuit of other people's wealth."

He rose. "And there's the whole story," he said. "Your men are at the door, Mr. Hennery. I imagine that Annie will be glad of your help by the time you get there. As for me—will you pardon me?—and give my thanks and my well wishes to the good woman to whom my existence has meant little besides trouble? The other cat, as I have been informed by Mr. Leeming, is in the safe of the *Leader* office, is it not? And my credentials . . ."

"Will be all right with Elliot," said Kym. "He knows most of the story now." Hennery walked toward the door where his men were waiting for his direction before picking up the pitiful body of Sandy Thompson. Karl Meisterberg joined them there after picking up the cat that stood so innocently and a little battered now, on the center table where Dawn had placed it.

For several minutes after the others had left them alone in the sun-filled quiet of Annie Thompson's front parlor Dawn and Kym did not speak. Then, rising from his chair and moving his long legs slowly toward her like a small boy who has been called to the teacher's desk, he stood above her.

He knew that he must call the office; he knew that he had the biggest batch of hot copy that had ever come his way, and that it was the chance of a lifetime to scoop every other paper in the city; and he knew that he must get his story into the ears of a re-write man before headquarters had time to give it to the *City Press*. But he knew, too, that he must do one other thing first.

"Slim," he said, looking down at the girl reporter with an expression that none of his fellow-workers would have recognized as belonging to hard-boiled Kymmerly, "I think maybe I'd better kiss you now."

About the Author

Eleanor Atkinson was born in July 1899 in Hinsdale, Illinois. Eleanor was the daughter of journalists and authors Francis Blake Atkinson and Eleanor Stackhouse Atkinson (most famed for the 1912 novel *Greyfriars Bobby*). Eleanor's sister, as Dorothy Blake, wrote magazine pieces and family novels *(The Diary of a Suburban Housewife* and *It's All in the Family)*. Eleanor married advertising copywriter George Wallace Cox in 1922, and had two children, Eleanor and Wallace (but soon divorced after her son was born). Her son was actor Wally Cox (1924-1973). Wally noted in one interview that his mother was nomadic, traveling around the country, and that he attended nine schools in twelve years. She wrote for a Chicago newspaper for ten years. As a journalist for a Detroit newspaper during prohibition, Eleanor wrote a feature story recounting her adventure first riding with a rum runner smuggling alcohol from Canada to Ohio, then joining the Coast Guard as they chased the smuggler. During the 1930s, she remarried, to Benson K. Pratt. Eleanor and her family lived in Omena, Michigan; the Omena-Northport area inspired the setting for *Death Down East*. Eleanor wrote two mysteries as well as regional novels (such as *Seed Time and Harvest)*. Eleanor died in West Nyack, New York, January 14, 1952.

COACHWHIPBOOKS.COM (PRINT)
COACHWHIP.COM (EPUB)

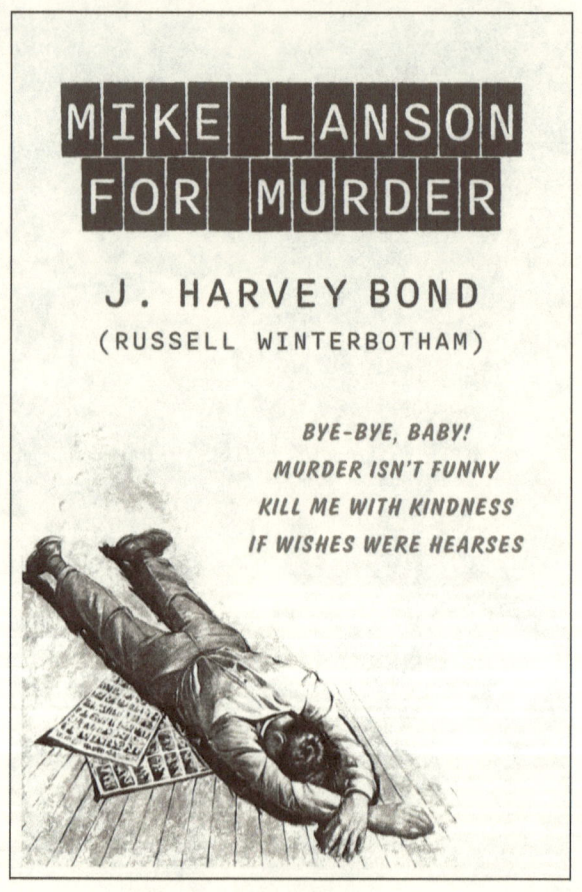

No Face to Murder

EDITH HOWIE

COACHWHIP PUBLICATIONS
ALSO AVAILABLE

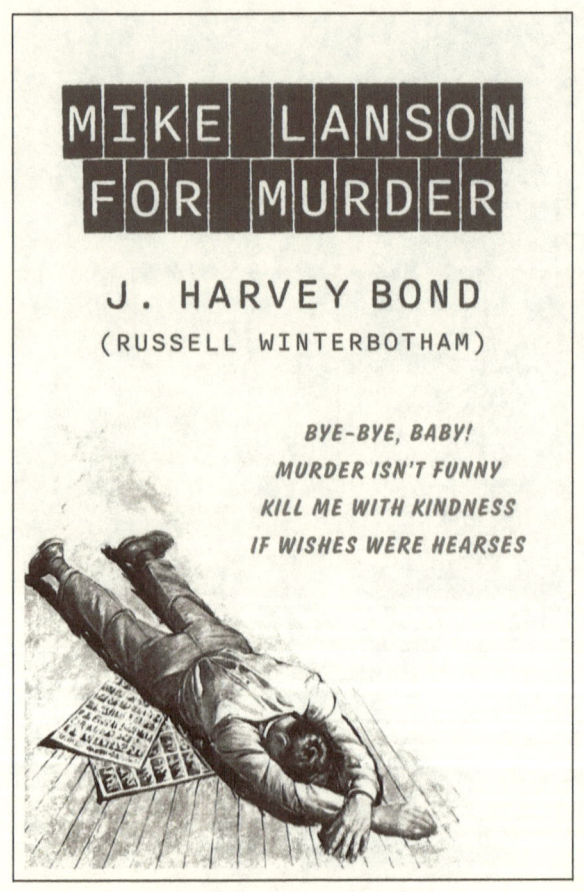

MIKE LANSON FOR MURDER

J. HARVEY BOND
(RUSSELL WINTERBOTHAM)

BYE-BYE, BABY!
MURDER ISN'T FUNNY
KILL ME WITH KINDNESS
IF WISHES WERE HEARSES

POISON CASE | MURDER CASE
NUMBER 10 | NUMBER 33

FROM THE FILES OF
THE MICHAEL JOYCE AGENCY

LOUIS CORNELL

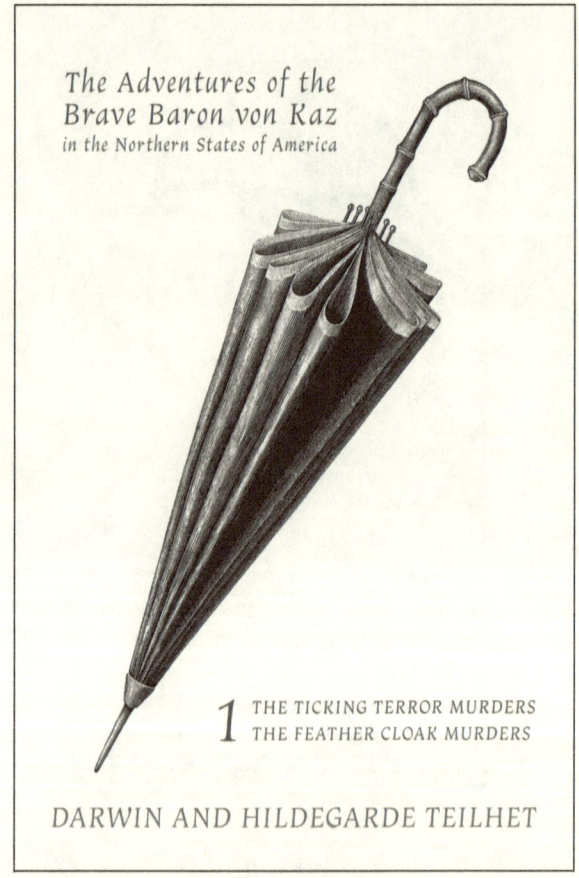

COACHWHIPBOOKS.COM (PRINT)
COACHWHIP.COM (EPUB)

www.ingramcontent.com/pod-product-compliance
Lightning Source LLC
Chambersburg PA
CBHW050427260626
47156CB00003B/1189